The Queen of Broken Hearts

Tobias International

Published in 2017 by FeedARead Publishing

British Library C.I.P.

A CIP catalogue record for this title is available from
the British Library.

Q💔 AUTHOR'S NOTE Q💔

Previously in the back of The Queen of Spades, the next book (this one) was introduced as being called The Queen of Hearts, but as I began writing it and the darkness began to fall once more, the title just didn't seem appropriate for what you and they are about to receive.

Therefore, let me introduce to you The Queen of Broken Hearts.

Prepare to be dragged to hell.

Now let us pray.

Tobias International ☺ xx

***

www.facebook.com/tobiasint
@tobiasint

For Bellie and for Timmy

You were the best dogs in the entire world
and I am so fortunate and so thankful that we
were able to share our lives together.

♥ I love and miss you both ♥

Also by Tobias International

Q♣ The Queen of Clubs Q♣

At the far end of town is Divas cabaret bar, filled with beautiful men, drag queens, desperation and lost hope.

Step into a world beyond your wildest dreams. What price are you prepared to pay for the success you crave so much? What price are you prepared to pay for love?

Watch your back. Reset your mind. Leave your paranoia at the door. How safe will you be when the warning bells begin to sound?

Welcome to the darkness.
Your secrets are safe... for now.

And

Q♠ The Queen of Spades Q♠

On the outskirts of town, in a house filled with cameras and secret doors, ten drag queens come together to compete in the ultimate social experiment.

With so much at stake and so much to gain, who can afford to take their fabulously drawn up eyes off the game?

But as jealousy and humiliation take over and the desire to win overrules, who will play fairly and who will be dealt a losing card?

And when the lights go back on, whose life changing plans will have suddenly taken an unexpected turn for the worst?

Keep your enemies close. Keep the truth even closer.

Q♣ PROLOGUE 1 Q♣

Previously in The Queen of Clubs

"...But first tonight, breaking news just in: A local man was knocked down by a car which then drove off at speed. The incident happened on East Green Street earlier today.

He was treated at the roadside for multiple injuries before being taken to the Royal City Hospital. He was pronounced dead upon arrival.

Police are appealing for witnesses or anyone with any information to contact them..."

Previously in The Queen of Clubs

Without hesitation, Wendy picked up the frail, limp body in her arms and carried it towards the exit, stepping over the stunning costumes she had so desperately wanted; just as another huge explosion imploded the building.

Both bodies fell down; Wendy landing on top, protecting Tequila from any further harm.

Ignoring her own pain, Wendy half dragged, half carried Tequila's body to safety on the street just as the fire engines began to arrive.

But there was no sign of life from Tequila.

Wendy pushed down on Tequila's heart and commenced the process of resuscitation.

You will live.

You will live.

But nothing happened. The body remained unresponsive.

Through tears and pain, she looked up. What a sight she must have appeared, with makeup streaked all down her face, skin blackened from the soot, no wig, no shoes, shredded tights, splattered blood and pain throughout.

She saw Oliver standing there, watching. The tears falling down his face too. But there was somebody else with him, or what looked to be somebody else, holding him tight from behind.

It looked like Jake...

But Jake was dead!

She looked back down at her lifeless son.

Damn it, another life will not be taken!

She began the process of resuscitation again, this time more determined than ever. Belief engulfed her entire body, mind and soul, just as it had done inside the building.

You will live!

You will live!

You must live...

My beautiful boy!

July, following the Divas fire

Chris Randall sat on the edge of the bottom bunk bed in his tiny prison cell listening very carefully for the sound of approaching footsteps coming towards him from any direction. All seemed silent around him.

Finally, he sensed he was all alone.

He stared hard at the whitewashed brick walls surrounding him where he had scratched his initials 'CR' into the wall in large letters.

He stared at the heavy closed door, now scuffed and bashed in places where previous occupants had possibly tried their hardest to break their way through; undoubtedly with no success.

The silver, metallic toilet and the water-stained hand basin in the corner of the room, which he continuously seemed to share with an endless queue of new cellmates, were both in need of a wipe down; although it was unlikely that a chambermaid of any description would ever arrive to undertake such menial tasks for him.

Nor, it seemed, would any of the other cellmates whose names he barely ever learnt, let alone care for any reason why they might be passing temporarily through his current residence.

On the inside, names and faces were very easily forgotten, but nicknames helped him remember.

There had been the Skinhead Nutter, who was always off his head on whatever illegal substances had been smuggled in that day; the Cry Baby, who greatly irritated him especially during the night when it was time to sleep, and more recently the Farter, who for obvious reasons he really hated.

It was most definitely a far cry from his previous life as the owner of Divas cabaret bar. The five star luxury, the champagne and the fine dining that he was more than accustomed to all seemed a lifetime ago now, but had actually only been a matter of a few weeks.

But in there, inside his Hellish torture chamber of sorts, it could have been longer. It certainly felt a lot longer.

Still, he didn't go without and he didn't struggle. He knew that if he scratched the backs of others they were more likely to scratch his too, and he had all the time in the world to earn favours, make his demands, lay down his law and dream about his freedom and everything that came with it.

Top Dog he was not, that was far too much effort, but he played the game sensibly and he knew the score. He knew how to win and he seized his opportunities to come out on top in other ways.

For this handsome, confident, business man alarmed a lot of the inmates in there and even some of the more timid and less witted prison officers.

The rest of them did not know how to take him and as a result of this he was generally left alone to his own devices which he was always extremely grateful for.

And that was exactly how he wanted it.

Initiating the new ones into his way of thinking was no longer his priority. He, and him alone, was his priority now; that and his freedom of course.

He stood up and stared out of the small window overlooking the concrete wilderness beyond. The evenings would still be very light for a long time yet, but the longest day had passed and the darkness was already slowly beginning to push its way forward and over more time to come, the long, light evenings would slowly fade and die.

Autumn would also begin to creep in on them and before anybody had even had the time to blink, the darkness would rule supreme once more. Leaves would desert their hosts and Halloween would soon arrive.

Halloween, a time when they say the veil between the living and the dead is at its thinnest strand. And who knows what ghosts from the past might be waiting in the wings to renounce themselves to an unexpected audience?

And then bonfire night would follow with all its colourful glory; insisting that everybody stops to take notice; demanding to be champion of the world; receiving every ounce of all the attention whilst claiming all of the victory.

Autumn was nature's very own firework display, but this year maybe, just maybe the vibrant floods of red and explosions of colours would be caused by some other means; some other substance; some other motivation that would draw the cold, lonely winter nights ever inward until they all slowly began to suffocate within the arms of its relentless power...

The prison officers had recently made their routine checks, and whilst he was confident they wouldn't be back again for a while, he still listened carefully for he had almost been caught out before.

He could not be caught out this time; there was too much to risk.

Now was the perfect opportunity for him to action his latest misdemeanours; for whilst he was alone in his cell he could undertake all manner of deceptions and actions.

He could still, albeit in a limited capacity, rule the outside world from in there and he had every intention of doing so for he still had his own little puppets to play with and, whether they liked it or not, he was controlling their strings.

He was the master of destinies and there was very little they or anybody else for that matter could do to stop him.

Very carefully and with exact military precision, his index finger and thumb slipped neatly into a tiny rip he had made in the lining of his thin, tired mattress. Together they easily located a small handheld device hidden safely within.

He pulled out a tiny, fully charged mobile flip phone and whilst doing so shuddered as he remembered the repulsive favour he had needed to fulfil in the shower block with a very overweight and somewhat rancid opportunist to get it.

He vowed never to subject himself to that again but on this occasion, it would be worth it in the long run.

Just as a final precautionary measure, he put his ear up against the cold metal covering on his cell door and once more listened very carefully. There still didn't seem to be anybody moving around in the corridor outside.

He returned to his bunk bed, quickly dialled a number and prepared to speak in a quiet, yet rushed manner.

"Hi, it's me, listen, do you know what you need to do? ... Good, just leave it a while yet, okay. Let the trail go cold, but soon, yes. I want him dead and I don't care how you go about doing it. Well, it's the least he deserves, isn't it? ... Yes, then you can have exactly what you want, you have my word on that one. Now, you're not going to flake out on me, are you? ... Good, I'm glad to hear it because I don't want to have to wait until I get out of here to do it myself."

Chris ended the call at that point and once again listened carefully at the door to ensure nobody was around before slipping the phone into the toilet.

It had served its purpose now and he didn't expect that he would need to use it again; although it would certainly have been a useful commodity to have kept and perhaps traded for something equally as useful.

He shoved it right into the u-bend and beyond before flushing any evidence of it ever being in his possession away.

He was not prepared to risk it being found during a random cell search.

He was not prepared to compromise extending his stay in there for any longer than was necessary.

As far as the inside government was concerned, he was a model guest and that was all they ever needed to know.

Settling down for the evening, he switched on the small television that always seemed to flicker slightly during the exciting bits, before plumping up his only pillow as best as he could and relaxing on his bottom bunk bed.

It was time to catch up with the ongoing reality TV saga that the media was calling 'The Black Queen' (AKA The Queen of Spades).

Ten drag queens.

One murder.

One bloody big mess.

He hadn't planned to watch it obsessively but one of the drag queens in there, a Miss Anna Phylactic, had mentioned in the first episode that she had competed in the Divas Beauty (drag) Queen contest that he himself had actually set up.

And even though he didn't remember her at all, from that moment on he was hooked to the show; as so it seemed was the rest of the prison and the entire viewing nation.

However, it was Miss Shimmy Shoo's wasp-tongued approach that had made her his firm favourite in there, although there was something about the born unlucky Miss Robyn RedBreasts that fascinated him too.

Like them, he was also under house arrest and he needed out.

And like their accommodation, the walls that currently housed him could not hold him for long.

But he would find his open door out of there and he knew that he would.

And Heaven help the world outside when that day arrived.

Q💔 CHAPTER 02 Q💔

Now forward to late October

It should have been the happiest day of her life, but that was far from her reality.

It should have been her wedding day, but the devastation down her dress and the destruction around her clearly advised that she had not walked down the aisle, hand in hand, with her one true love on the happiest day of her life.

Instead, here she was sitting all alone in her room in a comfortable, easy chair, the lamp barely casting any light over her tear-filled eyes.

What would become of the lovely presents that her family and friends had so carefully selected for her?

She would no longer be able to open the beautifully coloured ribbons and tear apart exquisite gift-wrap that covered new toasters and kettles and fine china.

They would probably all have to be returned, but she couldn't think about that now.

She felt too weak.

She felt too broken.

Her heart was destroyed.

Oh, the humiliation.

Her once stunning, crisp white dress was now as mascara covered as her face was. All ruined now, just like the gorgeous hair ringlets and French roll she'd had fashioned for her big day and to which she had tried to undo and release back into a flowing mane but with little success.

Nearby, music was playing a song for broken hearts and a tiered cake lay in ruins to her side. Her vibrant bouquet lay in tatters all around the tiny, white, lace-covered shoes she had so majestically slipped her luscious, little feet into.

She stared down at them as further tears fell to the floor.

This never should have happened; none of it. Why oh why had it come to this? She just couldn't understand.

She reached out for a handful of flowers and with tightly gripped hands began to destroy them even more than they were.

He loves me...

He loves me not....

He loves me...

He must love me! He must... he must... he must...

But he couldn't have loved her.

Why ever not?

How could he have done this to her? How could he humiliate her like this in front of all her family and friends? Hadn't they been happy together? Were they not destined to be together? Had it not been love at first sight?

So what had happened to result in this conclusion?

How could she face life alone now when it had taken her so many years to find this one?

She had hoped she would find somebody; somebody kind and tolerant, but this one had definitely broken all the moulds.

Now he had broken her heart.

Apparently, he loved every face and mask she showed the world.

'There were more opportunities to love all these guises' - that is what he'd always led her to believe.

And she had believed him.

She didn't believe him now though. How could she?

Man, if she ever laid hands on the mould that had made him, she would wedge an eight inch heel right through it. Maybe then, he might just start to understand how her heart felt right about then.

She pulled off her false eyelashes and placed them on the side table next to an expensive looking decanter of what appeared to be brandy.

Should she drink her sorrow away and drown away all the tears and the pain? Would that even help? A quarter-filled glass next to the decanter suggested that perhaps she had already made a start.

Was he not her Romeo? Had she not been his Juliet? Had he not hollered up to her balcony on more than one occasion?

How would she ever get over this? Could she get over this? Was her fate always destined to be this way? Destined to replicate the ill-fortune bestowed upon the real Juliet?

She thought about the lovely Oliver. Dear sweet Oliver. Is this how much his heart had hurt when Jake had passed away? Had he felt like self-destructing too just as she now felt?

My God, how could anyone face that much pain alone? How had that dear, sweet boy coped at the loss of his own one true love? How was he possibly coping even now?

She closed her eyes and dropped further back into her chair. An empty bottle of pills fell from within the ruffles and layers of her dress and rolled away across the floor, out of sight.

What had she done to deserve this? She didn't know. She couldn't recall. Was she slipping into a state of denial?

Was there any time left to save her?

Did she want to be saved? Her heart was broken beyond repair and what else was there to live for?

And all she could think about was Oliver and how he must have felt. Oh poor Oliver; that poor, poor boy. She was almost channelling him now; consumed by his despair and misery.

And the tears quickly fell down her makeup streaked face once again as she imagined how he must have been torn apart by the tragic death of Jake Robinson.

But who would miss her if she was gone? Not her once fiancé. Not now, not anymore, not ever, amen, that was for sure.

And what would life be without him in it? Nothing, that's what it would be; absolutely nothing.

In the distance she could hear a sound. The doorbell began to ring. Just once at first, then again, then over and over.

Was it him? Could it be him? Had he changed his mind? Did he want her back? Could she take him back? Was he still her one and only?

She stood up or at least tried to. Perhaps she would know her answer when she saw him face to face; when she was besotted once more by his manly features and when she had looked deep into his eyes.

She was pretty sure she could forgive him.

She stumbled and her legs gave way beneath her for they were weak. She was tangled up in her dress and couldn't help but fall backwards into her chair. It was too late, she was drifting away. The energy and the soul were leaving her body.

The doorbell continued to ring. The banging on the door began and quickly became relentless. She could hear him but barely. It was him. It was definitely him. He was back. He wanted her back. He needed her.

"I'm so sorry. I love you." But inside her head, his distant words were becoming implausible. "Please marry me today, just as we planned. Please say you'll be mine."

She needed him too, she really did, but she could barely move. The end was gently whispering her name.

She had so little strength left. She made one final effort to stand but she couldn't hold herself up. She fell heavily to the floor amongst the petals and the stalks.

This woman's work was done and dusted.

And with her final dying breath she said, "He loves me..."

And the sad, sad song stopped playing, all was silent and one Miss Wendy WolfWhistle lay motionless on the floor.

HERE WITHOUT YOU

You loved me once upon a time
Where did it all go wrong?
I'm lost in thoughts from way back then
I'm lost in eyes I may not see again
I know I'm still in love with you
I wonder if you ever think of me

Without you
Now I know how long a day can be
Without you
If only I had found the strength to become the
person I could be
Now I am here all alone
Without you

You left me once upon a time
I never thought you would
Forever is the longest time
To never think of anyone but you
Together we were everything
But everything to you was not enough

Without you
Now I know how long the night can be
Without you
If only I had found the time to listen to my
heart
Now I am here all alone
Without you

If only I had tried
When you were crying deep inside
Now I am dying deep inside
Without you

So I sit waiting - waiting here for you
At a table set for two
Hoping that, the roads that took you from me
Will one day, bring you safely back to me
Back to the arms of my love

Without you
Now I know how empty life can be
Without you
If only I had been the person that you needed
me to be
Now I am here all alone
Without you

If only I had tried
When you were crying deep inside
Now I am dying deep inside
Without you

Without you
Without you

Oliver stood behind the bar at The Queen's Legs cabaret bar and tutted in disgust as Wendy picked herself up from the cabaret stage floor and stood tall and proud in her ruined wedding dress.

Amongst the ripped up flowers and the ruined cake, she bowed and curtsied to the appreciative audience who had certainly enjoyed her opening theatrical number; her very own rendition of the *Dying Swan*.

Originally, she had insisted upon performing a ballet in a crisp white tutu that had once belonged to that woman that some pudding had been named after, but the line of reality had to be drawn somewhere.

It turned out that her not dancing and not singing was the compromise to maintaining the harmony between herself and her son slash drag queen daughter Miss Tequila ShockingBird who was also very keen to own the limelight and had not necessarily wanted to share any of it with anybody.

Oliver shook his head in horror as the crowd continued to applaud and cheer the success of her debut performance, and he watched as she flung flower petals over herself like it was confetti.

Seriously, had there not been enough death in his lifetime already without seeing it acted out on the stage in front of him in his new workplace and a hundred or so other people, all of whom had probably by now forgotten all about Jake and all that had previously happened.

Still, it wasn't about what he did or didn't want, it was all about the punters and they were certainly getting their money's worth that evening inside The Queen's Legs.

It was in fact the first night of The Queen's Legs being open and whilst the place was heaving from corner to corset, he felt very out of place there serving behind that bar.

Of course, he would have hated it even more if he had known that Wendy was actually pulling on what she had perceived to be Oliver's own real life emotions to enhance her own performance.

But still, if nothing else, the audience had loved it. They had remained silent throughout as Wendy had played the jilted bride whilst giving the performance of her career.

And as Martin Taylor-Smith, the owner of the new cabaret bar, encouraged the audience to give her one final round of applause; they willingly did so as she took one final bow and flung the few remaining flower petals that she could grasp hold off into the air before departing the stage for a costume change.

Finally she had made it, and if she could make it here she could make it anywhere, and poor, deluded Wendy WolfWhistle was already thinking beyond her very own limited limitations.

But for the punters, it had been months since Divas cabaret bar and all its controversy had burnt down, but now there were drag queens and live cabaret back in their lives; to say nothing of a brand new venue right on their very own doorsteps.

For many of them lived on East Green Street where The Queen's Legs was situated and they had all been waiting desperately for this night to arrive.

And to have this exciting, new venue right on the corner of their road was a dream come true for most; although many would still undoubtedly require taxies for the short-journey home.

Martin stood facing them as the curtains behind him closed so the stage could be cleared for the next act. All eyes were on him and he hoped he could continue to maintain the momentum, his composure and his confidence.

But it wasn't easy knowing what he knew and wondering whether everybody there knew his secrets. For when you have secrets, you can't help but wonder if everybody else knows it or suspects it or is questioning your every move.

You can't help but spend your days and nights worrying that you might unnecessarily spill the truth at any moment, whether intentionally or otherwise.

You can't help but forever watch your back or forever watch who is coming around the next corner for you.

Known to some but unknown to most, Martin had been quickly removed from the police force just after the Divas cabaret bar fire, but in some ways it had been a welcome relief.

He had sold his Mother's house and with all the money she had left him, he had been able to finance the opening of his very own cabaret bar and it was this new venture that he had hidden within. But the truth being - he had really screwed up big time and there would never be another chance to go back.

Oh Christ, had he locked his office before he came out on stage?

Prying eyes could potentially cause some real problems for him; regardless of how innocent their curiosity may seem.

But this was his life now and the truth would out sooner or later and it would greatly affect them all.

Yes, as soon as he got off this stage, he would have to check his office was definitely locked. Annoyingly, it was starting to become a bit of an obsessive habit of his, but nobody could find out what he knew.

But The Queen's Legs was supposed to be a new start; a place perhaps where he could be comfortable and be himself; a place where he would appear less invisible to the viewing world around him.

Yet, even as he stood there on the stage in his smart, new suit, with the microphone in his hand hosting the show, it still didn't feel as though anybody was looking at him or taking him seriously or even listening.

He felt very far removed from being the star host of his very own show.

But they must be listening to him because he had asked for a further round of applause for Wendy and she had been given it. They had heard that.

Hmmm, but what else might they have heard?

Oh, the paranoia of a troubled past.

Is this how Chris Randall had felt, night after night, at Divas cabaret bar?

Back then when he was a paying customer or equivalent, he hadn't appreciated all the pressure from the demands and needs of the paying public.

From their perception, they had worked hard all week and deserved a good night out. Is that what this was? Was it a good night out? It certainly seemed to be. Well, so far anyway.

He was enjoying himself, even if the terrified look on his face said otherwise.

He glanced over to the bar staff who were given a moment of grace whilst the attention was drawn away from the bar. He noticed how uncomfortable and ill at ease Oliver seemed to be. Thank goodness there were at least two of them feeling like that.

Martin knew that this had not been the right environment to put Oliver in but he couldn't help but persuade him into working part time behind the bar.

But as Oliver had willingly consented to it, it was now out of his hands.

The verbal contract had been agreed. And all contracts were binding.

The reasoning for Oliver's decision was unknown but he was there nonetheless and Martin very much remained unconvinced by the young man's motives for doing so.

Wayne, the former landlord of The Maiden's Jugs pub where The Queen's Legs now stood, in comparison seemed more at ease behind the bar and with undertaking the necessary supervisory roles that went with running the place.

Wendy and Martin were both clueless about running a pub but he had the expertise and knowledge they required and, when all was said and done, Wayne had an open mind that wondered aimlessly and Wendy had had nothing but good things to say about him when Martin had suggested getting him on board.

Of course, Wayne had needed to leave his home though, but that had been expected for this was no longer his business.

However, it was quite unknown how he had really felt about any of this. Maybe he was pleased, more than likely he was not, but his own business had failed and at least he could make ends meet now.

Martin, firmly holding the microphone in his slightly trembling right hand, put away his reservations and addressed the audience once more.

They were looking at him, directly at him and they seemed to be listening to him too.

Why would they not be? He had gained their full attention.

"Welcome to the grand opening of The Queen's Legs," he said, and as the words came out his confidence came out too. "It is wonderful to see so many of you here with us tonight.

"In just a very short while we will have more cabaret for you; the debut performance from our very own Miss Tequila ShockingBird but first I would like to tell you about next week's Halloween, charity masked ball. Tickets are available from behind the bar and it would be great to see you all there too hidden behind your masks."

"Are the rumours true?" shouted a voice in the crowd, and momentarily Martin began to fear the worst.

"Rumours?" he almost whispered back, dreading the response.

What did they know?

"About the special guest appearance?" said the same voice in the crowd.

"I reckon it is," replied another.

Martin breathed a sigh of relief, gasped it almost. "Yes," he replied, this time without any insecurity, "the rumours are true. There will be a very special guest appearance from 'The Black Queen', but who that is, remains a secret."

Martin left the stage and the punters returned to their drinks and discussions, particularly about who the guest appearance would be from.

Everybody had had their favourite character in the show and the fact that one of them would be setting foot in their brand new venue was too overwhelming for some to comprehend.

What with her terrifying manner and blood-soaked dress sense, Miss Camp-Isla Bacta seemed the most likely one to make a Halloween guest appearance, but in theory it could be any of them and it didn't really matter which one it was for they were all loved by somebody.

Meanwhile back at the bar, Oliver was putting together quite a large drinks order for a group of lads who had just arrived. He turned to Wayne as he was opening a bottle of dry white wine. "What's 'The Black Queen'?" he asked and was surprised at the response from both his work colleague and those who were standing nearby.

"It was only the best drag queen reality TV show ever made that didn't star Ru Paul," replied Wayne, and a few of the others around them nodded and acknowledged their agreement.

"Oh, I didn't watch it," said Oliver, putting down the bottle on the bar before reaching for several wine glasses.

"You honestly didn't watch 'The Black Queen'?" questioned Wayne, "or as it was also known: 'The Queen of Spades'?"

"No, I really didn't. But actually thinking about it, I may have heard it mentioned on the

TV or somewhere, perhaps in a magazine. It is ringing a bell."

"Ten drag queens, one murder, one bloody big mess. Oh my God, it was compulsive viewing. I thought everybody had watched it."

"When was it on?"

"About July time, I can't believe you didn't watch it. In fact, there was even footage from Divas during the drag queen beauty..."

Wayne paused, realising that he had mentioned a name that nobody should ever dare speak of in front of him. "Oops. Sorry about that."

"It's okay," said Oliver, "you can mention it. It happened. I can't change the past, nor do I really want to forget it... not yet anyway."

"But Martin said I wasn't to speak of it when you were around."

"Wayne, honestly it's okay. I can't ignore it forever."

And as Wayne quickly told him how Divas had linked into the show, Oliver knew he couldn't ignore it forever.

And if the truth be known, he actually intended to address it imminently. He put down the last of the drinks order on the bar and rang it through the till.

The group of lads carried their drinks away leaving, for the first time in quite a while, a gap at the bar between the people and himself. And for the first time in quite a while Oliver could actually see across the venue.

It was only then that he noticed a youngish chap on the far side, sitting facing him and staring right back; although whoever he was immediately looked away the moment he realised he'd been spotted.

Oliver was slightly unsettled by this, but it went with the territory. People stared at the barmen, maybe even lusted after them too. Heaven knows he himself had done just that at Divas cabaret bar.

And then he was thinking all about Jake again.

He looked briefly back at the youngish chap who had been staring at him but didn't notice anything in particular about him. He had a cap pulled down low over his face and his hair and fringe were pulled forward in the style of an American teenage heart-throb. His whole body language was quite closed off.

Still feeling quite uncomfortable by his presence, Oliver turned to Wayne and gestured discreetly towards this mysterious person. "When did he come in?" he whispered.

"Why do you fancy your chances?"

"Don't be daft. There's something about him that's bothering me. He's just been sitting there staring at me. At least I think he has. But he isn't anymore."

"Leave it to me," said Wayne, picking up a wet cloth from underneath the bar. "I'll clear some tables around him and see what I can find out for you. Believe me, if somebody is after you, I will be the first one to know about it."

Oliver watched Wayne randomly working his way through the crowd and towards the youngish chap whilst collecting a couple of glasses here and there on the way. He wiped down the table nearest to him and then returned back to the bar area.

"I said hello to him," explained Wayne, putting down the empty glasses on top of the bar, "but he was quite unresponsive. I said I was Wayne and he muttered something back."

"What did he say?"

"Well, I think he said his name was Jay or something that sounded like Jay if not."

"Jake? Did he say Jake?" questioned Oliver without a moment's hesitation to what he was actually saying out loud.

"He may have said that," replied Wayne, shrugging it off.

Oliver looked back across the room to where he had been sitting, but Jay or whatever he was called had gone.

It couldn't have been Jake, could it?

Surely he would have recognised him?

Surely he would have come right over to the bar and spoken to him?

Jake would not have ignored him, right?

Jesus, what was he thinking?

And it was just thinking; wishful thinking.

How on Earth could it have been Jake?

How on Earth could Wayne have spoken to him?

For Jake was dead.

Q💔 CHAPTER 04 Q💔

Martin stood on the stage once more with his microphone in hand, a now much calmer hand, and addressed the crowd of eager faces in front of him.

Hmmm, had he locked his office? He really must check... again.

"If you've loved it so far, believe me you have not seen anything yet. Please welcome on stage for the very first time tonight in her grand debut performance down here at The Queen's Legs, our very own Miss Tequila ShockingBird."

Martin stepped out of the way and dashed straight to his office where he discovered his office door was tightly locked... again.

Phew.

And so the music started and Tequila appeared on stage amongst a thick haze of shimmery smoke that quickly began to fade.

She was an absolute stunning vision in shining silver grey from head to toe.

An absolute treat to behold and this divine creature was so ready for her close up.

Finally, here she was, headlining the show.

Okay, admittedly sharing the spotlight with her Father slash drag queen Mother Wendy but it was her Tequila who was the real dancer, the wafer thin, the eye candy of the show. This was her moment and she was about to relish every moment of it.

To her, Wendy was nothing more than just a back-up and fill in to her own exceptional talent and creative direction.

♫ *I'm ready for my close up*
I'm ready to be swarmed by all the boys
If you want a taste of honey
Then you'd better earn the money
Cos my best things in life don't come for free ♫

She couldn't help but stare out at the crowd and smile wildly. This was exactly what she had wanted; this moment of pure self obsession, self loving and self desire.

She felt utterly beautiful in her outfit but more than anything, she loved that she was the centre of their absolute attention. She was their world and she was sitting right on the top of it.

Nobody was drinking and nobody spoke. They were spellbound by her presence.

♫ *I'm bitching with my best girls*
We're hanging out with all the mighty fines
If you think that you can buy me
Then I reckon you should try me
But if you can't, then get out of my way

That's right, tonight...
If you can't then get out of my way ♫

My God this feeling was amazing. Self indulgence had never felt so good. And to think Chris Randall had promised her all of this at Divas cabaret bar and then never delivered. She was foolish to think that he ever would have.

Thankfully, she had never stepped in too deep where that one was concerned. However, that was very easy to say now and in hindsight.

Chris Randall had never given her anything like this. He had promised to fulfil her wildest dreams but just like him, his words were empty and meaningless.

She had been willing to pay for the success she had craved so much but a price was never given; although the real cost would very soon be known to her.

♫ *Cos sex sells, sex sells*
You can use me and abuse me
If you can flash the cash
Cos sex sells, sex sells ♫

She couldn't wait for the musical bridge after the third verse where she knew the audience would go wild for her. And as Martin had accurately announced, this audience had not seen anything yet and they would demand more from her.

No, not demand more... beg for it.

And she would enjoy every moment. She would have them eating from the palms of her hands. But then many of them already were.

And to think she had had almost died in the Divas fire and missed all of this. But that really wasn't worth thinking about now because she intended to live forever.

♫ *New age wealth is so obscene*
But Baby that's my dream ♫

Ha, damn you Chris Randall and your new age wealth. I hope you rot in Hell or wherever it is that you've been dragged to.

But somebody like Chris Randall still had their uses and irrespective of whether it had all fallen flat once before, it was not to say that opportunities may not come forth again for those who needed to seek them out.

> ♫ I want to call my agent
> I must insist all my demands are met
> If you're freaking with me, Baby
> Then I'm tweaking with you, maybe
> I'm wreaking havoc everywhere I go
>
> That's right, tonight...
> I'm wreaking havoc everywhere I go
>
> Cos sex sells, sex sells ♫

There was no better feeling than any of this. And Divas very own Miss Connie Lingus, or whatever it was she went on to call herself, had been the perfect inspiration for this particular little routine.

Hmmm, whatever happened to that sex selling, drug taking, talentless bitch?

Oh, who cares? Her reign was over months ago. She, and all those who sailed on her, could rot in whatever Hell she had dragged herself off to as well.

Now it was her turn to rule the land of drag-believe.

Okay, so having Wendy WolfWhistle as one's Father was not ideal but when the cards were on the table, Wendy had saved her life from the Divas cabaret bar fire and had been able to make James/Tequila joint-headliner of their very own cabaret show to which Tequila had very much enjoyed having a lot of creative input with.

Wendy was still the lazy, fat, not good for much, deluded has been drag queen who abandoned him and his Mother just weeks after he was born so he could live in a dress for the rest of his life, but this had definitely helped make up for some of that.

Fickle he most definitely was, vengeful not so much. And they both had a nice place to live too, above the pub with Martin. It wasn't ideal, as his bedroom was a tiny box room, but it was comfortable and it more than beat sleeping backstage at Divas or in a hospital bed where he had been recuperating for quite some time.

One day soon he would have to face his Father demons but at the moment his attention was focussed elsewhere.

At the moment he was Tequila, all eyes were on her and the musical bridge was just about to follow...

> ♫ *I need a cash advancement*
> *I need more money than we first agreed*
> *Now that I'm a superstar*
> *I will be who do you think you are?*
> *Cos I'm the best you're ever gonna get*
>
> *I'm the best you're ever gonna get...* ♫

And as though right on cue, the doors of The Queen's Legs cabaret bar burst open and four burly policemen in perfectly fitted trousers and handsome faces stormed inside, one after the other, knocking over drinks, tables and the occasional gay man who had been unable to move out of their way in time, or had quickly stood up hoping for a quick frisk.

The audience generally were quite bemused by all of this. The ones who had had drinks spilt over them slightly less so but the sight of one handsome man in uniform after another entering the building soon calmed down their annoyance.

Tequila stood on the stage and tried to make out what was going on, but the bright lights shining down on her were dazzling her and obscuring the view.

The music continued playing but the venue was filled with the stomping of their heavy, manly boots on the wooden floor beneath their heavy steps.

The first policeman reached the stage. "James Davies also known as Miss Tequila ShockingBird?" he asked the anxious-looking drag queen in front of him.

"Yes," she nervously replied.

"I am arresting you on suspicion of previously drug dealing at Divas cabaret bar. You do not have to say anything but it may harm your defence if you do not mention when questioned something you later rely on in court, anything you do say may be given in evidence."

Tequila stood there motionless whilst she was handcuffed and swarmed by all the boys.

She was led off the stage and through the crowd of shocked and surprised faces.

Was this the close up she had so eagerly been expecting?

"What's going on? What are you doing?" screamed Wendy running onto the stage in an over-stretched, glittery leotard, before catapulting herself onto the wooden floor and then falling head over tit as one of her ill-fitting high heels buckled inwards under her weight; her wig of course also flying off in true Wendy style.

Helpless and sprawled out legs a limbo, a bald headed Wendy lay across the floor, reaching out for nothing but air, watching as Tequila was led away, out of the venue and out of sight.

Had there been spilt beer underneath her, it would have been just like the olden days down at Divas cabaret bar.

The confused audience looked at each other and then suddenly burst into applause and cheers. What a fantastic show this was turning out to be. What a cracking opening night. Their expectations had more than been met, in fact they were beyond exceeded.

This place was so much better than Divas cabaret bar ever had been.

Some of them couldn't wait to personally congratulate Tequila on her literally show-stopping performance when she returned, hopefully with the uniformed hired policemen in tow.

Endless selfies would be requested and social media would be instantly plastered with her success and all manner of Tequila hash tags.

Back at work, everybody would say what a great night it had been, what a totally hash tag fabulicious show and what a pity the people they were telling hadn't been there to see it for themselves.

Some of them hoped that the policemen were strippers or suchlike and would soon be back showing off their truncheons and handcuffs to all and sundry.

But Tequila didn't return and the policemen were not strippers or suchlike and they would not be returning either.

This is not what they had rehearsed.

This is not what should have happened.

This was not part of the show.

Sometime around mid-October

What had happened to Mark (AKA Miss Connie Lingus) is that some four or so months earlier and on the very same night of the Divas fire, he had quickly, and without leaving any trail behind him, fled from what they had often described (especially Jake) as that god-forsaken town; taking with him just the bare essentials for his new life someplace else.

Nobody knew where he was, where he had gone or what he had done.

It was not really known that it had been him who had created so much devastation that night and had so carelessly risked all their lives in the process.

Although in all honesty, Chris Randall probably suspected what had happened and what Mark's role in it had been. In fact, he probably more than suspected what had happened and he had probably spent a long time in prison, alone in his cell, thinking it all through, over and over, again and again, until he couldn't bear not being able to do a single thing about it.

But Mark was safe now.

And all was well for Mark now.

And he did not look back.

Well, sort of...

But what was an absolute definite for Mark is that his alter-ego Miss Connie Lingus, who he now despised more than words could ever explain, was no more; along with every wig, shoe, scrap of makeup, false eyelash and exquisite gown she had owned; most of which were destroyed in the Divas fire.

Yes, Connie was never ever allowed to come out and play again.

It was a pity that he had had to run to his freedom so quickly. If there had been more time maybe he could have re-instated his website and sold the lot to Wendy WolfWhistle; claiming that it had once all belonged to that really famous girl group who had done really well on that singing reality TV show.

Still, it was not as though he needed the money anymore. He had more money than he ever imagined he could have; even if none of it started off as his own; even if he had had to endure that wretched life up to that point.

For now he was very happily living off the proceeds of Chris's misfortunes and would be able to do so for a very long time indeed. Well, it was only what Chris owed him in compensation for damaging his life.

Finally he was free of his past and he could be anybody he wanted to be, although all he really wanted was just to be known and appreciated as Mark.

Gone too were the breast implants that the punters used to love and had once paid generously to explore. In their place, a flat, manly chest had returned, albeit with two notable scars but the chest hairs that now grew around them were doing a reasonable job of covering them up.

In time, he hoped he would barely notice them anymore as he fully accepted that they were part of who he once was. And for the first time in his life, he was beginning to like what he saw in the mirror.

He had let his shaved hair grow back and he no longer needed to shave several times a day. In fact, he quite liked having stubble. It was the new him. For once in his life, he actually felt attractive and thought that perhaps others may think the same too.

For once in his life, he actually saw a future for himself as Mark.

And his past as a money-grabbing, drugged up, dragged up whore with nothing but broken dreams and an unquenchable thirst for both his next quick fix and revenge had been obliterated in the Divas fire with the rest of the dreadful memories he had lived with for so long.

Now he was able to live his life freely, reset the button and start again; just as he had often hoped he might. And with Chris safely locked up in prison, hopefully forever for what that bastard had done to them all, he was beginning to build the foundations of a new existence where he could rise again; this time headlining his own life – however it turned out to be.

Yes, this phoenix was determined to rise from the ashes he had caused.

That is if life let him, of course.

And back to July

The prison door opened quickly and widely and the tall, stern prison officer with the seventies inspired moustache ushered Chris out of his cell.

"You have a visitor, Randall," was about all he could muster up in a way of an explanation for the disturbance.

Chris had been waiting patiently for this visit. This was all part of his survival plan and he intended to manipulate every ounce of the situation. It was all part of a much bigger action plan that would require careful monitoring and consideration, but he knew he could make it work and he would.

There were too many out there who had wronged him or at least had tried to and they needed to suffer. They would all be punished under the Law of Randall.

Line up the soldiers and shoot them all down.

Unfortunately, this was potentially everybody that Chris had ever met, but some definitely deserved it much more than others, but they would all get theirs when the time was right. Nobody would be exempt. Exceptional circumstances would not apply.

Chris followed 'Moustache' through the labyrinth of corridors towards the visitor's room; with one security door after another being opened with just a quick flash of some sort of smart card against an electronic wall-mounted device.

Oh what Chris would do if he could get hold of one of those cards, although rumour had it that there were already some in circulation amongst the prisoners, but that was hear say and possibly not too likely, but who really knew what was going on with these four walls?

Chris didn't mind 'Moustache'. Despite his facial exterior, he was one of the nicer officers in there; not fanciable but generally okay. Better than most of the others though.

Chris spotted his visitor before they saw him. They had their head down as though they did not want to be seen. They certainly did not want to be there, that was for sure.

Chris smiled politely as he sat down opposite him at the small, wooden table. "Well, hello," he said to his visitor. "Good to see you again."

Understandably, the pleasantries were not returned in any shape or form. Instead his visitor shuffled uncomfortably in his chair and tried to lay his eyes on anything other than the person sitting in front of him.

Good to see each other again? It was far from that.

If he had any other choice he would be anywhere but there, but he didn't have any choice, did he? In all honestly, this was a person who he hoped he would never have to see again.

This was a person who he had hoped their paths were never destined to cross again, but yet here they both were, sitting face to face, and Chris Randall, damn him, was holding the winning cards: a victorious royal flush in comparison to his queen high.

And Chris Randall, screw him, was holding all the cards, every last one. And each card would tell its own story and each card was bound for somebody.

The Ace of Spades, the Ten of Diamonds, maybe even the Tower of Destruction...

Maybe his card would be the Queen of Broken Hearts?

"So what do you want?" he abruptly asked his host, who despite his current situation was reigning supreme as the ultimate leader of the pack.

The King of Clubs, perhaps?

Their eyes met once more, and Chris ensured they stayed there, fixed and rigid for as long as possible. He wanted to stare right into the windows of his soul with his cold blue eyes and freeze him inside out starting from his very core.

He momentarily folded his arms, thereby building a barrier between them both, so only the eyes and the gaze were dominant. The mouth remained motionless.

The staring eyes said it all.

His visitor couldn't bear it any longer and distracted himself with a notice board in the distance, the unfriendly interior design and a cobweb on a light fitting slightly to the left of where Chris was sitting. Anything was better than looking directly at his host.

"I suppose you are wondering why I asked you here."

"You hardly asked me here, did you?" replied his visitor, staring momentarily at Chris's chin as it seemed the least obtrusive of all of his facial features; although his gaze quickly returned to the notice board in the distance.

"You can't even look at me, can you?"

"Of course I can't," he replied. "Why would I want to?"

"You need to remember that I know what you did. I know exactly what happened. I know all about you."

His visitor shrugged it all off. In a way, this was not the worst thing. The nightmares and the restless nights that had drowned what should have been his sweet sleep for so many nights had been worse than this. This was not the worst thing, the anticipation of his past catching up with him had been worse.

The fear and the dread that Chris would catch up with him one day had been rehearsed during so many sleepless nights, but being here now, confronting him, awaiting his destiny, was not the worst thing. It was almost a relief to be in this situation.

And whilst he had hoped that their paths would never cross again, he always knew that they would.

He always knew that Chris would bide his time and summon him when the time was right. He just hadn't expected it to be so soon.

Clearly prison was giving him ample opportunity to compile a plan of revenge.

"What exactly do you know?" replied his visitor.

"I know you have done me wrong," he calmly explained. "I know that you have things that I want. I know that these walls can't hold me forever. Take your pick, which one do you like the sound of the most?"

His visitor stared down at the ground, at his own footwear, at the table legs and the hard, faded red, plastic chair he was perched uncomfortably upon.

"Well?" said Chris.

"None of them," he quietly responded.

"To be honest with you," replied Chris, "I couldn't care less what you think. You screwed me over and this is what we are going to do about it."

His visitor listened carefully to every single word spoken and did not enjoy hearing any part of it.

"No," he bravely responded once Chris had finished his well-prepared and overly rehearsed speech.

Chris stared coolly back at him and once more ensured he captured his gaze. This was the response he had expected, but it was not the outcome he knew he would finally receive in the end.

Chris always got what he wanted. He knew that this time, like all the others, would be no exception to the precedence he had already set so many times before.

"No," responded his visitor again.

Chris stared back at him. Although not speaking a single word, his silence said everything that required hearing.

He folded his arms again, tighter than he had done before and continued to stare. He once again reiterated his demands.

"And let's suppose I agree to this..."

"Which you will," interrupted Chris.

"What will I get in return?"

"This will all go away for you. I may even go away for you too. Wouldn't you like that?"

His visitor sat silently for a few moments, trying his hardest to stare at him in the eyes.

If he could do that then he could do this.

Finally he nodded. It was a no-win situation whichever way he cut the cake, but the thought of Chris never crossing his path again seemed a possibility that he felt had to be the journey he needed to take.

"It's been a pleasure," said Chris standing up and neatly pushing his chair back underneath the table.

Anything that made him look good in the eyes of the prison officers had to be a bonus for him.

He continued to speak: "Now if you'll excuse me, I want to get back to my guest accommodations, the next episode of 'The Black Queen' will be on soon and I don't want to miss it, it's very addictive."

His visitor stared back at him, unable to think of anything to say in return to that.

"Believe me, it's the only thing getting me through this summer; well, that and this of course. I just hope my new cellmate doesn't disturb me. He farts all the time. As you can probably imagine, I've nicknamed him the Farter, still he's better than the other two; one was a skinhead nutter and the other kept crying. God, he was really annoying."

His visitor watched Chris gleefully leave the visitor's room, knowing he was about to lose everything that he had planned so hard to put into place.

And annoyingly, Chris had been able to come along and take it all from him so easily too.

Damn him, this world would be a much better place without the likes of Chris Randall in it.

In all honesty, who would ever really miss the likes of Chris Randall?

For he was an unnatural, obnoxious, evil, sinister, twisted mind who was nothing more than a blemish on any landscape that had the misfortune to have him associated with it.

Seriously, why couldn't somebody just come along, line him up and shoot him down dead?

Was there any reason why Chris Randall, even just for once in his life, couldn't be dealt the wretched Queen of Broken Hearts, just for a change?

But maybe this time he would.

Forward to late October

A day or so after the grand opening night at The Queens Legs, Oliver felt as though he was finally ready to start facing his past.

He always knew he would have to sooner or later and now seemed to be as good a time as any to do so.

He had tried to put everything to the back of his mind but keeping it so tightly locked up inside him was not healthy and it was deeply affecting him every day.

He locked the door to the one bedroom flat that he had almost given up and had briefly shared with Jake for just a few days, left the apartment block, and headed off up East Green Street, zipping up his jacket against the autumnal weather as he walked.

This time, he headed in the opposite direction from The Queen's Legs cabaret bar. His destination was to the other end of town, the part where nobody seemed to visit anymore.

He needed to see Divas again, or what was left of it. He had not been back there for months; not since that fateful night and he needed to cleanse his mind. He needed to address what was in his head so he could start to heal; otherwise he felt he would never move on.

He tried to avoid making eye contact with the section of road where Jake had been knocked over and killed, but it was inevitable that he would look.

He would always look.

He would always need to look, for it was a genuine if not horrific memory of their time together.

Whilst he had morbid fascination, he would never lose the memory of the love they once shared.

A ribbon was still tied around the lamp post where Oliver had once left flowers. The flowers had long since gone, but the ribbon had remained. On it Oliver had written: Jake RIP - Always be with me.

It had been hard not going to the funeral. It was even harder not knowing where it had been held or where Jake's body now lay or where his ashes may have been scattered.

He had waited in that hospital for so bloody long only to be told nothing. He hadn't been able to see him. He had not been allowed entry beyond the pale blue chairs in the waiting room. He recalled the smell, the old magazines which brought very little comfort or distraction and the fake plants with the realistic dead bits.

Eventually Martin had spoken to him. Jake's family had been contacted and at their request the body had been immediately moved. The funeral was held where they lived. They finally had their son back even if it was no longer him.

The funeral had only been for close family. Martin explained that he had tried to tell them about his relationship with Oliver, but they were not interested. His Mother, like the twin boys and his younger sister were all too distraught to listen. Their darling Jake was dead, that's all they heard. That's all they needed to learn.

Maybe if the circumstances had been different then they might have listened. If they had known how deep and pure their love had been for each other then surely they would not have left him out. But as a result of what had happened, all that now remained physically for Oliver was a ribbon tied around a lamp post which he had written his farewell message to Jake on.

It was barely even a start to saying goodbye to the love of his life.

And as he walked towards the other end of town, his heart felt heavy once again and he needed to blink away the tears on more than one occasion.

If anybody cared enough to stop him and to ask if he was okay, he would tell them that the chilly autumn breeze was blowing directly into his face making his eyes water; although in all honesty, he didn't really expect anybody to stop and ask if he was okay.

But nobody ever cared to stop him and to ask if he was okay, not anymore, for his mood was constantly dark.

A wall was now built around him were love once lived. His emotions were erratic and understandably he was furious at the world and the system and the police and the hospital and anybody who had stood in his way or even dared just to be happy in front of him.

He was furious with Jake's family and with Chris Randall too, particularly Chris Randall. He hoped their paths would never need to cross again.

He thought about working behind the bar. In all honesty, he had not wanted to work at The Queen's Legs. He had only recently returned to his day job after an extended period of compassionate leave which he knew he had been lucky to be given as he had not been there that long. But Martin had been relentless in asking him and eventually convinced him that it might help with the whole moving on process.

And in one way or another, being behind a bar did seem to make him feel that little bit closer to Jake.

He passed the lesbian bar just down the road from where Divas had so grandly stood. He saw the canopy of the run-down, tired looking newsagents that he had once stood underneath whilst he summoned up the courage to go inside Divas that very first time, and then he finally saw where Divas cabaret bar had been.

Now it was covered up with scaffolding and wooden barriers and work had commenced to restore it.

Higher up though, there was evidence of the fire, bricks were black from the smoke and windows remained smashed. It was just a shell of its former glorious and rather amazing self.

He remembered Martin holding open the door for him and then later making a play for him. He remembered how he had stayed behind for late night drinks with Chris and how Jake had desperately asked him to do so. He certainly remembered the fire, although he didn't know how it had started.

He was trembling as he recalled the flames and the thick, black, bellowing smoke and the anger in his eyes as he confronted Chris in the dressing room.

In a strange way this was all helping.

In a strange way the past was moving further away from him.

They had all left through the back entrance that night and around the side and back onto the pavement where he now stood.

There was no chance of going around the side now though as, like the rest of it, it was boarded up too.

He had avoided this part of town for so long now, partly due to fear, partly due to avoidance but he quickly realised that it couldn't hurt him anymore. It was just a desolate, ruined building that no longer had a soul.

Granted, it would one day be something else and over time people may say 'Didn't this used to be a drag queen bar?', but the very foundations and the walls and the rafters and the roof tiles would all belong to something else, where happier memories would be made.

One day, this building would be somebody else's dream and Divas cabaret bar would be a very distant memory.

But that night.

That awful, awful night.

He was standing here.

Right about here; just where he was standing now.

What was he trying to remember?

Wendy had carried Tequila out of the building before trying to resuscitate the life back into the weak, unresponsive body, but that wasn't it.

It seemed that there were sirens going off everywhere and thick black smoke bellowing high into the sky. Everything seemed to move in slow motion, just like in the movies, but that wasn't it.

What was his mind trying to ask him to recall?

Wendy had looked up at him and he was crying.

It had been hard not to cry after everything that had just happened. When the adrenaline had been that high, there was only one way the emotions could go, and that was down.

Before trying to awaken Tequila once more, Wendy had looked up at him and she looked surprised, but why?

Why?

Why?

Suddenly, as though the memory had formed in his head, he remembered what he felt he needed to know. There had been a presence behind him, warming him momentarily, keeping him safe and then disappearing.

But who was it?

And as he stood there, staring at what was left of that night and the ruins of the place he had once loved more than anywhere else in the world; somebody approached him from behind and put their arms around him tightly and rested the side of their head on his back right between his shoulder blades, just like had happened on that night.

To Oliver, this person felt familiar and smelt familiar and the hug was comfortable and familiar.

And then they whispered softly into his ear. "Oliver, this really was the last place on Earth I ever expected to see you standing in front of."

And now... a short intermission

"Hi there, I'm Miss Shimmy Shoo and you probably best know me from starring in 'The Black Queen'.

"Since leaving the house I have been so busy being absolutely gorgeous around the whole wide world that I barely even know what day it is anymore.

"And I know exactly what you're thinking: How does she stay so fresh looking? Her skin is immaculate.

"Well, let me tell you my secret. I use *Shine* from my brand new beauty range *Made by Shimmy Shoo*. It cleanses, it moisturises and it even polishes those hard to reach areas that nobody dares ever speak of.

"And as for those little bags of skin under tired eyes, well, *Shine* will just shoo them right away.

"*Made by Shimmy Shoo* is available in participating retailers now, whilst stocks last.

"Don't forget, if you want to look as natural and beautiful as me then use *Shine* because you can never have enough shoo polish on your face."

Still late October

Oliver took his Mother to the old fashioned tea room where the staff looked at least twenty years older than they probably were.

It was the first time he had been there in months. It had been his and Jake's favourite hangout; a place where they could meet in safety and talk openly and honestly. A place where he had felt the staff were really rooting for them.

Maybe they weren't even the same staff anymore.

There didn't seem any point in going there anymore; not without Jake, but with his Mother at his side he felt safe and comfortable being there and it certainly seemed like a day to continue to face the demons of his past.

After collecting their order, Oliver set down the tea tray of hot drinks and cakes on the table within the window bay where he and Jake always used to sit.

"Please don't think that it's not nice to see you because it really is, but I still don't understand why you are here."

"Oliver," she replied, picking up her steaming hot mug of coffee, "I'm worried about you, even more so since I just saw you standing outside that wretched building. Has that place not caused you enough grief in your life already?"

"It's the first time I've been back there," he explained, lifting up his hot drink to his mouth and blowing gently onto it. "I just needed to see it again, that's all."

His Mother took a much needed drink from her cup before she continued to speak. "What with everything that has happened here, I do wish you would reconsider coming back home. Even just for a little while?"

"But this is my home now," he replied, helping himself to the biggest piece of cake because that is what Jake would have done. "My job is here and my friends. I have a little part-time job in a cabaret bar too. I'm moving on or at least I'm trying to."

"I'm sure you are but I have to tell you, I stayed in a hotel yesterday and I visited that little cabaret bar last night and I'm not happy about you being there. Naturally and from your descriptions in the past, I spotted that Wendy WolfWhistle person immediately."

"It's not so bad," remarked Oliver, fearing he was yet again fighting this losing battle but knew that he needed to stay strong if he was ever to win this war.

He couldn't leave this town, not yet; at least not until he was ready to and he was far from that.

"Oliver, I heard that a drag queen was arrested there for selling drugs. Four policemen raided the place whilst he erm she was performing to a song about prostitution."

"Well, it would sound bad when you put it like that," he replied. "Anyway, we don't know she did it for sure. She has been released pending further investigation. Anyway, she wasn't selling them there if she did do it, it was at Divas."

"Don't be flippant, Oliver. And whilst on the subject, I have also heard rumours since being here that Divas may have been burnt down by another drag queen. Is that true?"

"I don't know who burnt down Divas. A drag queen, did you say? Anyway, who is telling you all of this?" he questioned, slightly bemused by her sudden intake of gossip.

My God, after just one night in a nearby hotel and now she was the local grapevine.

"Oliver, I want you to think very carefully about a fly that is so fascinated by a light bulb shining so brightly that it will eventually be burnt and killed by it."

"What? I don't understand what you are trying to say. Are you calling me a fly or a... What?"

"And then this morning," continued his Mother quickly and firmly, "I find you standing outside that very building or at least what is left of it as though it is the most natural thing in the world to do. It is like you are permanently looking for trouble."

"I just wanted to think about Jake."

"I understand that, but your obsession with that place nearly burnt you once. I mean, it could have killed you."

Oliver nodded, she was absolutely right, but he needed to do what he needed to do and this particular day he had to go and see what was left of Divas.

"Sweetheart, I really don't think you being here alone is good for you. Will you at least consider moving back home? You were going to before."

"But that was part of a different plan," choked out Oliver sadly, and he felt that he might cry again. "That was a plan for me and Jake, but there is no me and Jake now."

Oliver looked at his Mother as she drank in silence and he blinked away the pending tears he could feel forming in the corners of his eyes.

He knew she worried about him and understandably so. He knew she didn't trust this town or the people in it, but the only real enemy was Chris Randall and he was firmly locked away behind bars.

Everybody here was his friend; everybody here was on his side. He had no reason at all to believe that his safety was in jeopardy anymore.

"I will think about leaving," he finally said, but rather unconvincingly.

And they both knew he probably wouldn't and that further excuses would come when the issue was broached again.

"But aren't you lonely here?"

Oliver thought about this for a few moments. He was lonely and there was no denying that but whilst he was here he still felt close to Jake and that stopped him feeling entirely alone.

"Okay," he replied, this time more positively, "I will consider moving back or at least leaving here, but it needs to be when I'm ready to leave and I'm not ready to leave Jake's memory yet."

And as he said it, his eyes filled up once more and several tears had already rolled down his face before he had any chance of stopping them. It had been a turbulent, eventful and absolutely terrifying year and still he couldn't let go.

His Mother stared at him. She would continue to keep her eye on him, her only son. He was very dear to her and she loved him very much and whilst she was not happy that he wouldn't come back with her, she knew she must respect his decision. She knew he would always need her, this year more than ever and maybe the next one too.

Maybe in time, she could share the journey of fixing him with another but there wouldn't be another Jake, and the possibility of another loved one for her son seemed a lifetime away yet.

However, this impromptu trip to see him had revealed everything she had suspected. All was not as fine as he had attempted to make out on the telephone.

It was easy to try and fool a person by putting on a very brave voice but when standing face to face with each other, the truth was much harder to conceal.

"I will continue to come here and see you up until which time I am convinced that you are okay," she said. "And I may not always tell you when that will be, so you had better be prepared, my son."

"Thank you," he replied and he realised for the first time in a long time to what extent he had been hiding his real feelings about everything that had happened.

And he no longer needed to feel so alone for he wasn't alone. He never had been.

"But I will tell you one thing," his Mother continued to say, "I have a bad feeling about you being here and until proven otherwise, I personally would not trust anybody here and I think you should do the same."

"I'll be fine. Honestly, it will all be okay. You'll see."

"Hmmm, well, just stay in regular contact with me and let me be the judge of that. And if anything and I mean anything changes, you contact me immediately. Have I made myself clear?"

Oliver nodded for there was no defying his Mother when she was in this mood and in all fairness it was a very fair compromise from both sides.

"Now this cake looks lovely," she said changing the subject.

And with that she tucked into the delicious slice of chocolate fudge gateau that Oliver had chosen for her before asking him how work was going and whether he was keeping on top of his bills.

But she still wasn't happy even though her face showed otherwise.

Something was going to happen, she just didn't know what or when.

But she felt it and she feared it and it was not going to be good and she was very concerned that Oliver would be the one to bear the consequences.

And for the sake of any further disagreement, let's call this one a Mother's intuition.

Still late October

James (AKA Tequila) was struggling to sleep.

He was glad that his recent ordeal with the police was now behind him and he was glad that it had all been dropped due to a lack of evidence. But the whole experience had been most upsetting.

The reality of what had happened and what might have happened was terrifying and one that he did not want to endure again.

After all, prison was for people like Chris Randall, not for him though.

Maybe for Wendy or Connie too, but definitely not for him.

He was so annoyed with himself. How could such silly decisions have been made previously? Honestly, selling drugs for Chris in Divas was so stupid. What had he been thinking? Had he been that desperate to get to the top?

And whilst he was glad that was over now, he would not be glad if he knew that the background that had led to this unfortunate incident was far from done.

And he would also not be glad to know that the unfortunate incident was very much a warning not to be ignored.

James had also run up all those massive debts too once he had started at Divas and they had so far never been paid back either.

He had tried to live the same champagne lifestyle that Chris thrived upon, but alas he had soon discovered that he could ill-afford to do it himself.

He was far from being champagne Chris, he was barely even cava Chris.

Nobody had come after him yet about those debts, possibly nobody had been able to find him, but he constantly lived in fear that sooner or later some sort of debt collecting company or psycho man with a giant hammer would catch up with him, and when that day arrived it would not be pretty.

It was true what they said: you can run from your past but it will always catch up with you sooner or later.

Shock... would they take his new mobile phone off him towards payment?

Oh buggar, he really hoped not. He had only just pinned all his apps in the correct logical order on the home screen.

But he needed a massive financial injection just in case and that was no lie. He just needed to win big on a scratch card or for somebody to give him a load of cash and the only person he knew that that was ever likely to come from was Chris. But that really wasn't worth thinking about because he knew what Chris would want in exchange.

It's what Chris always wanted in exchange: Blood, tears, sweat and an audit trail that never came back to him.

James had foolishly trusted him in the past and had done as he had been asked. Chris had promised to give him the things he most desired and look what had happened there.

Damn him and his cabaret bar.

James was glad it had burnt down

Hmmm, Divas was completely destroyed in the fire.

It must have been insured though...

There would have been an insurance payout; possibly a massive payout. Chris would not have overlooked having that in place; no matter how dire his situation had been back then.

Chris wouldn't need all that insurance money though... Not yet anyway. Not where he was.

"No, James," he quickly told himself out loud. "Not after the last time."

Chris had ruined too many lives as it was. That man was an automatic thunderstorm waiting to devastate all that he touched. He would not destroy this though; not now, not anymore.

And just for a moment James felt indestructible, but it didn't last for long and within just a few seconds the reality hit hard again.

What could he do to get some more money?

Perhaps Martin would give him a pay rise?

But he had already asked for one and had point blank been refused.

But he was, after all, the star (the joint star) of the show, and the punters were spending frivolously to see Miss Tequila ShockingBird (and Wendy) night after night.

He (they) was (were) a huge success and that must be worth more money in anybody's pocket, especially his. I mean what else could happen, it's not like Tittie or Connie would ever turn up and reclaim their spotlight.

Well, they better hadn't, otherwise he would have to shoot them down hard if they even contemplated the possibility. This was his gig now and he would fight to keep it and he was far from done with fighting.

James switched on the tiny lamp that sat on the tiny cabinet at the side of what felt like his tiny bed, climbed out from underneath the duvet and stared into the mirror at the half-dressed young man with barely one eye open trying hard to look back at him. It was not pretty; especially the hippopotamus-sized yawn that followed.

He would sneak downstairs and help himself to a shot of whisky or brandy and then come back up to bed. That might help him sleep.

Out on the landing, he could hear both Wendy and Martin snoring from their respective bedrooms; my God no wonder he was struggling to sleep, although in all fairness their snoring wasn't the problem.

Using the flashlight on his mobile phone to guide the way, James tiptoed down the stairs, taking care not to step on a particular step half way down that creaked slightly.

He didn't want to wake anybody; especially Martin who tried to watch those optics and measures like a hawk. A small drop of something would probably go unmissed but it wasn't worth adding petrol to the fire and letting Martin know it was happening on a regular basis and who had done it.

He would probably think it was Wendy anyway.

Ha! He did the last time.

Downstairs, the bar area was eerily quiet. The flashlight was run along the bottles until one bottle in particular caught his eye.

Mmmm *Southern Comfort*; yes, that would do very nicely.

And it did do very nicely too, as did the second one and the packet of cheese and onion crisps that was also quickly consumed.

Okay, stop now James.

But James did not feel even slightly tired anymore and although he knew he should go back to bed and try to sleep, he wasn't ready to go back just yet. Perhaps he could watch a little bit of television upstairs? But no, he didn't want to do that either.

He left the bar area and shone the phone light towards the stage, greatly appreciating the view that the audience must have when they watched him performing as Tequila.

Oddly, James or his alter-ego never drunk Tequila, but often did think of him/herself as glorious as a sunrise.

No thank you to the slammer though!

He had never been inside Martin's office; tucked away backstage well away from the noise and the bar, the crowds and the cabaret. He didn't know if anybody had. They were under strict instruction not to go in there, never to go in there, unless they were supervised by the man himself.

He really hadn't ever wanted to go in there anyway as it was not his thing. Dancing and gorgeous outfits and long rounds of applause were his thing; particularly the long rounds of applause.

But business-related things though... yawn!

Ooh but that might work. That might help him sleep.

Business-related things... yes, huge yawn.

In fact, he could feel himself yawning at just the very thought of it. Spreadsheets and Word documents and contracts and things... no thank you.

Yaaaawwwwnnnnn....

James wasn't sure if the door would even open; it would probably be locked; if they weren't allowed in then it should probably be locked, shouldn't it?

He had seen Martin lock it many times before; even when he was just nipping to the toilet or to make a nice cup of tea. This should be no exception.

But much to his surprise, Martin had made an error and the door opened and in went James. He sat himself down at Martin's desk on his executive, leather-effect, black swivel chair with up and down capabilities and back readjustment that had clearly been purchased with the fuller figure in mind.

This had been so careless of Martin. Rest assured, in the morning when he discovered it was unlocked, this mistake was not bound to be repeated.

Being in here alone was a once in a lifetime opportunity. Oooh what would he find? What was Martin so particular about hiding?

He switched on the desk light and stared into the flat, dark and lifeless computer screen which had been turned off some hours beforehand.

There was not a spreadsheet or equivalent in sight. There was something rather dull on a white board on the wall but James was not clever enough to know what any of the coloured lines even meant, even though there was a colour coded key at the bottom.

He tried to interpret the data... Well, the red highlighter pen must be used for something that is different from the green one, and... yawn.

And there it was, the yawns had returned.

James moved his focus to a set of in and out trays on the desk which had labels on such as 'Post in' and 'Invoices to be paid'.

Nothing of interest to be seen there.

Hmmm, nothing of interest to be seen anywhere.

Hooray, at this rate sleep would become him in just a matter of a few minutes or less.

There were three drawers down the right side of the desk, the bottom drawer was slightly bigger, but it was locked. The other two opened; one contained some stationery and a tin labelled 'petty cash'; the other was empty.

Natural instinct and curiosity both kicked in and James opened the tin. It had once contained an exclusive range of chocolate biscuits but they had long been eaten, probably by Wendy.

There were several receipts inside it and a few bits and bobs of cash, but nothing that would even stir the contemplation of knocking it off for a better life somewhere else.

However, there was something else of interest in there though. A small, metal key was just poking into view underneath a clean five pound note, but the key for where; the bottom drawer perhaps?

Yes!

And now sleep was most definitely off the business–related things agenda, for there was a whole bundle of paperwork to browse through.

Paperwork that needed to be locked away, admittedly not very well, but perhaps Martin never anticipated that a trusted employee and housemate (even the one allocated to the tiniest bedroom even after much protesting and flouncy tantrums) would go through it in the middle of the night when he couldn't sleep.

The bundle was carefully lifted out of the drawer for James did not want to give the impression that anybody other than Martin had ever been through them.

Oooh, what would he find? He'd better not find out that Wendy was being paid more money for those mediocre, not quite lip-syncing in sync routines and not all that great really performances she insisted on throttling out on the stage each night when most people seemed to go to the bar or the toilet.

He carefully flicked through Martin's secrets with the flippancy of a bored seven year old during school holidays.

No, no, yawn, no, no, nope, yawn, no, boring, not interested in this.

Oooh, what's this?

He pulled out a smaller pile that had been fastened together with a paper clip and quickly put down the rest of the bundle, clearly remembering the place where this had been extracted from so it could be replaced without arousing any suspicion.

Oh!

Oooh!

Yikes!

Ouch!

He read through the contents of the entire smaller pile several times. He needed to make sure that he fully understood what this meant, the implications of the information he had just absorbed and the required strategy moving forward to ensure this enhanced his own life in one way or another.

Well actually he didn't so much with that intention but more so with the goal in mind that what he thought he had read he had actually read and how much cash this might be worth to keep his big gob shut.

He really hadn't seen this one coming at all.

Oh dear, Martin – this is not what you want.

And right then, James knew it would be a long time before even the slightest of yawns returned as his mind worked overtime to digest this information.

But when all was said and done, what did this secret actually mean for any of them, because surely it wouldn't just impact on Martin?

It would affect them all.

Sooner or later.

Still late October

Martin was sitting in his office moving paperwork from one side of his desk to the other. He was very good at doing that.

He was very good at making it seem as though he knew exactly what he was doing, but he didn't, far from it. But to the unsuspecting eye, he seemed to be on top of things.

He was far from being the ultimate business man. He wasn't designed for this type of work. He was better at what he used to do. He was better in the police force but those days were over now. This is what he did now.

Thankfully Wayne was always on hand to help with this, that and the other. He really was a God-send as he knew how to do things like order from the brewery, change barrels and put the rubbish out.

He stared down at the desk drawers and opened the drawer he hated the most. He took out the pile of documents that Tequila had gone through the night before, but couldn't summon up the strength to look through them again.

He was tired of looking at them and thinking about them and he thought about them a lot.

Sometimes he hoped it was all a dream and that one day he would wake up and it would all have gone away.

But it never went away.

And he didn't know that James (AKA Tequila) now knew his secret and was biding his time before bringing it to light.

For it was most definitely something he didn't want anybody to know about, especially his staff.

Sighing regretfully at the bad decisions he had made, he quickly stuffed the paperwork back into the desk drawer and closed it just as Wendy came charging into the room in full drag; this time with a heightened appetite for bright, yellow eye shadow and tight black hot pants that was very much like forcing two great Oaks into adjacent drainpipes.

He didn't want her to see the paperwork; he didn't even want anybody to know that there was paperwork to see. He certainly didn't want anybody to find what was in there and go through it.

He had very foolishly left his office unlocked the night before. He didn't know how it had happened, but he had been the first one up that morning so he seemed to have got away with it, or so he thought.

That wouldn't happen again though; the stakes were too high and there was too much to risk.

"What do you want, Wendy?" he asked, quickly glancing down at the drawer to make sure it was as closed as tightly as it could be.

He then regretted doing so in case Wendy noticed where his eyes had moved to, but she didn't notice what he had done at all, for her mind and her intentions, as usual, were too pre-occupied elsewhere.

"I think we need to talk again," she said, closing the door quietly behind her before gently pulling a chair forward, perching herself delicately down on it, with legs graciously slanted to the side and hands resting gently upon her lap.

Martin watched as she slammed shut the door as though a hurricane had blown through, grab a chair which she scraped right across the floor, hitting a flipchart and his desk en route, before sitting down with the force of ten wrecking balls, farting loudly in the process with hands all over the crotch area, which may or may not have been safely tucked away.

"Okay," he finally said, "what do you want to talk about?"

He often found himself having the same conversations with Wendy, time and time again. Hopefully this time it wasn't about the glass cabinet that they should have which would display all the exquisite accessories she had bought along the way that had once belonged to all the top celebrities, for example the old shopping basket that Toto had sat in, the chipped cup and saucer with the hand-painted periwinkles or Queen Elizabeth's chastity belt.

He knew and she knew that one day, she hoped to be so famous that she too would be able to donate her own personal crap to a similar cause.

Or perhaps to an emerging drag queen star, just as she had once been, that was in need of a wig that had been lacquered backwards so often that it had developed its very own bald patch, or a laddered pair of tights with only the tiniest of skid marks in them, or a pair of high heels with a very wonky undertone.

But that day was not this day, and Wendy still needed all those things.

"I want to talk to you about Oliver," she replied to him, although he sensed she was probably already thinking about her latest eau de toilette or as the rest of the world called it: bleach.

"What about Oliver," he replied slightly uninterested.

This too was another conversation that they often seemed to have and was also beginning to wear thin.

"I'm still worried about him," she replied. "I don't think him working behind the bar is the best thing for him."

"It was his decision to do it."

"After a lot of persuasion from you."

"Not that much."

"Seriously, you were like a man on a mission. You were not going to take no for an answer."

"He's young and cute; just what people want to look at when they're out drinking; much more so than Wayne anyway. No disrespect intended there, I know he's your friend but you have to agree he's no oil painting."

"I have never really understood that concept," said Wendy, adjusting her wig as it had come forward too much.

She pulled it back and it caught one of her false eyelashes on the way, pulling it right off. She didn't notice and would probably go out on stage looking like that. "All the oil paintings I've ever seen have been of badly dressed, goofy faced old spinsters with an unnatural desire to stare."

Martin smiled and let her ramble on in this way, for he knew that if she returned to the original subject then the conversation would take a very different direction, for it usually always did.

And it was a direction he no longer wished to journey along.

"If I was an oil painting," continued Wendy, "I would be stunning; just like the moaning Lisa."

Martin stared at her and braced himself for what was coming. He sensed that the digression was over and she would return to the subject of Oliver once more.

Maybe he could distract her with a chocolate éclair, or at least give her the money to go to the shop to buy one.

"Anyway," continued Wendy once more, "back to Oliver. Martin, I really think I should tell him what I know. He deserves to know."

Martin was firm in his response. "Wendy, no, we have been over this before."

"But it might give him hope."

"I hear what you are saying, Wendy, but what you think you saw the night that Divas burnt down was not what you saw. I'm telling you he wasn't there."

"But I saw Jake standing there behind him. I know I did."

"You were grief-stricken," explained Martin. "And you had inhaled a lot of smoke rescuing Tequila from the burning building. You were distracted by saving your son's life."

This time it was Wendy who was firm with the response. "I know what I saw and I saw Jake hugging Oliver."

"You're wrong," said Martin, "I was there too, don't forget. Jake was not there. Wendy, Jake is dead. His family took his body away and held his funeral."

"Then what did I see that night?" asked Wendy. "Tell me that?"

"I don't know what you saw, but what you think you saw was not Jake. Did you see him again?"

Wendy shook her head. No, she hadn't seen him again. Saving Tequila's life had been her key priority. The next time she looked up, there were police and fire services everywhere and paramedics dashing towards them to take over.

By this time, Tequila was breathing again and Jake was nowhere to be seen; if indeed it had been Jake who had been standing there.

Unless it was a ghost?

Could it have been a ghost?

Maybe Martin was right. Maybe the situation that night had caused the mind to play tricks on her. In that case, it was probably best not to say anything to Oliver.

Now stop being silly, Wendy, she told herself. Now think about lovely, swirly, girly things like gift receipts, Alice bands and tinsel covered ponies.

Oh, where has my false eyelash gone?

And Martin breathed a silent sigh of relief to himself. Wendy was back to doing what she did best and the conversation was well and truly over.

But maybe it wasn't quite over...

For outside his office, on the other side of the door, stood Tequila and she had been listening very carefully; collecting further ammunition, trying hard to fit together the pieces of the jigsaw; until she was almost ready to explode.

Secret paperwork inside a drawer, in an office, that was nearly always locked.

Wendy, very much believing she had seen Jake standing behind Oliver on the night of the Divas fire; several weeks after he had been knocked down on East Green Street and killed.

Martin, adamant that she had not seen Jake as his family had taken his body away for the funeral.

Martin, desperate to get Oliver working behind the bar.

What did it all mean?

Did it even mean anything?

Oh, and now she had a Tequila headache.

Still late October

Mark (AKA Connie) had escaped to the south coast; a place where he felt more than invigorated. A place where the only thing he was addictively obsessed by was inhaling lashings of fresh sea air.

He enjoyed walking on the beach and through communal gardens and for the first time in what may have been forever, he allowed himself time to not only stop and smell a whole army of different flowers, but to admire their beauty and their existence and to learn their names.

He enjoyed a problem-free life without ties and commitments and restraints.

His life was now completely and utterly stress free.

Well, sort of...

True, he would have to settle down into something sooner or later but that was for another day and not for now. For now he had just one thing to do and that was to enjoy his life and being a man of leisure each and every day. That was his routine.

Of course, after what had happened to Jake who knew how long any of them had left.

Who knew what was waiting just around the next corner for any of them?

And if Chris had his way, Mark would be a high priority.

Yes, the south coast was absolutely the right decision for him. He wanted to settle there for he loved being there so much.

He didn't ever want to leave.

He couldn't go back, he couldn't ever go back.

Not to that God- forsaken town.

But what if his previous life called him back?

What if it slowly began to peck away at him, day after day?

What if it began to eat him up alive like a cancer?

What then?

No, he would never leave; although a few nights previously he had stayed over in central London and that had been a very brave move for him.

And whilst he very much liked London and had often enjoyed visiting there in the past, and whilst it was a place where he felt he could just be another unknown face lost in the crowd in every shop and on every street and on the Underground, there was too much going on all the time to ever feel the need to settle there.

There was too much temptation; too many parties; too many opportunities to slip recklessly or without warning back into his old ways. And as his affirmation for life were reiterated: he couldn't ever go back.

Besides, he knew that London would not make him happy; not like the coast made him happy.

And whilst he was in London, he visited the theatre.

He didn't particularly enjoy the theatre and he knew he wouldn't actually stay all the way through the performance, but that evening he had good intentions and it was something he just felt he had to do.

His very soul had driven him to do it even though he had spent several sleepless nights fighting the urge. For his previous co-star who he had once shared the stage with, Divas very own Miss Tittie Mansag was performing in a touring play.

He had seen the posters in his new hometown as the play toured through. He had even read about it in a local publication and had immediately recognised the slightly larger than life man behind the former mask; there had been no denying who it was for they had sat side by side in a dressing room both as men and women for long enough.

In the end, he decided not to see the play where he lived but to go to another place and see it.

Although very unlikely, he couldn't risk being seen by Tittie and possibly word getting back to those that must not know where he was.

He felt he could trust Tittie though and whilst in London, he had debated at length whether he should present himself to the stage door or the dressing room or at least to a member of staff who worked there informing them that an acquaintance of his, from a previous life, was in the play and could he go backstage and wish him well.

Maybe even take a bouquet of flowers too; after all, isn't that what people in the arts tended to do?

Although when he was in the arts as Connie, nobody ever gave her anything as sweet as that. Nobody really gave her anything other than that which caused turmoil to any already unstable situation.

In the end he didn't present himself anywhere. He chose not to meet him, albeit even just to say hello. He just wanted to make sure that Tittie was safe and happy in his new life away from Divas, doing what he loved to do the most; perform.

But why he wanted to know this he was most unsure of. But it wasn't going back and he would never call it that; it was just a quick health check on a current situation.

The aftermath of Divas must surely have left broken hearts and scars across those he had been closest to and he was partly to blame for that.

He was a lot to blame for that!

If he had been more involved, more aware, less demanding of his own situation then maybe things would have been different.

And maybe Jake would still be alive.

Maybe...

Hmmm, his involvement in that one was very debatable.

No, he was not to blame.

Right?

Maybe the pressure he had put on Chris had led to his irrational behaviour.

Perhaps he just needed to completely clear his conscience before he could truly move on with his own life. Potentially, the guilt of his radical actions was the real driving force behind it all.

Maybe this once cold-hearted bitch was thawing out.

So it was with this mindset in place that he had sent himself to London to track down Tittie and his touring play or as he was now calling himself, and probably what he had always been called before he was recklessly hidden away inside Divas as Tittie: Parker Frampton.

And Parker did look happy and gave, for as much as Mark could bear to watch, a professional and convincing performance.

He was definitely not Tittie and he was definitely not George as he had also been known as back in that God-forsaken town. He was just himself; free from the horrors of his own past too. Unaware that part of his past was even there watching him.

Evidently, the endless nights of putting on Tittie and then wiping her away were very much a thing of the past. For it was a strong-abled and confident man that stood on that stage, blinded by different raging, stage lights giving the best performance he could.

Tittie had been able to move on with his life post Divas, perhaps he could too.

He knew he could.

He certainly wanted to.

Providing of course that the past allowed itself to be tightly sealed away forever and he didn't ever have to go back.

Because he could never go back.

Unfortunately, he already sensed that the winds of change were pulling him back in that direction.

THE WINDS OF CHANGE

The winds of change are blowing through
Can you feel that something's moving in that
wasn't there before?
Can you sense that there's a tension in the
air?
Are you concerned that things may never be
the same?

Well, you threw caution to the wind
And ripped my life apart
Now you've had your final chance with me

So let the waves break free from the shore
Because I don't want you anymore
Not even for a final goodbye kiss

I'll ride this storm for one last time
Knowing you're no longer mine
And so I pray...
Hoping that the winds of change will blow you
far away

The winds of change are roaring now
Across the ocean wide the mighty tempest
ever rages
And all around the lightning flashes through
the sky
And the thunder crashes through the
turbulence

Well, you threw caution to the wind
And played a dangerous game
And now things can never be the same again

So let the waves break free from the shore
Because I don't want you anymore
Not even for a final farewell day

I'll ride this storm for one last time
Knowing you're no longer mine

And so I pray...
Demanding that the winds of change will blow
you far away

Severe weather warning!
The winds of change are biting at your skin
Trying everything they can to pull you in

Danger levels rising!
Your courage and your future are
disappearing out of sight
The winds of change are drowning you tonight

You're drowning now
You're breathless now
There's no way out
Somehow, you must escape the winds of
change

And so I pray...
Desperate for the winds of change to blow you
far away

Q❦ CHAPTER 12 Q❦

Still late October

Inside his prison cell, all alone as he generally always was, Chris Randall sensed the pending changes that would sweep the compound.

He wasn't involved but he had heard the rumours and he knew that mass destruction was on its way.

It seemed as though there were forever hushed words and secret discussions in the corners of corridors and rooms that the prison officers tended not to patrol as often as they should.

Secret discussions that immediately ceased the moment the wrong person entered the space around them, him included.

There was a constant flood of knowing looks and well-timed glances that could only possibly mean one thing; the prisoners were planning their revolt. The House of Randall was about to collapse and there was nothing he could do to stop it.

But he didn't want to stop it.

He needed out of there and the sooner the better. He needed to be free of the four walls that forever held him hostage and which forever felt as though they were closing in on him until he could barely breathe.

He just needed to find that open door.

He needed to flee the endless noise of slamming doors and obeying the relentless rules and regulations that he had never written and to which finding loopholes in seemed impossible.

But mostly and more importantly, he needed to escape the deafening screams of despair in the middle of the night that always kept him awake.

Sometimes they were his.

Sitting down on the bottom bunk, he stared hard at the television screen in front of him. It was switched off but he could see his own reflection staring worryingly back at himself.

When had he become the star of his own reality TV show?

Audience ratings – one!

Prison was so much harder than he ever thought it would be. If only he had made different choices in his recent past. If only he had made different choices always.

Jake!

Oliver!

Divas!

He should have seen it coming, all of it. He should have foreseen the nightmares that would follow.

They were bad decisions, really bad decisions. And he hadn't considered any of the consequences.

Heaven forbid he should ever take responsibility for his own actions.

For in one way or another they had all led him to this, to the gates of Hell and beyond and he was drowning without a lifeline.

How could he have been so stupid to let them lead him here; to this; to this miserable and restricted life?

How could he have let himself be dragged to his Hell?

This was no life, certainly not for him. It was barely an existence. At any moment of the day, somebody in authority would tell him what to do or a bell would sound telling him it was time to do something or to eat or to crap or to take in the air for a short while until that pissing bell rang again.

He had lost complete control of his life and he needed that control. It was the very core of who he was and how he was. Without it he could never truly rule the world.

But soon, and he knew it was coming because he recognised all the signs, somebody different would tell him what to do and the sound of bells would ring harder and faster and louder than ever before, but this time they would be ringing for a different reason.

And then everything had the possibility to be different.

And if he had been dragged to his Hell, then somebody else should experience it too.

31st October - Halloween

Oliver and Wayne both stood behind the bar at The Queen's Legs cabaret bar and braced themselves for another hectic night.

It was the evening of the Halloween charity masked ball and the turnout was yet again immense; to the point where the venue was bursting at the seams and anybody without a ticket was being turned away; no exceptions to the rule.

Possibly because the venue was still brand sparklingly new and people were far from being tired of it.

Maybe because the previous police raid was still the talk of the town.

But mostly because the gorgeous Miss Lolita Lollypop from 'The Black Queen' was making a personal appearance there that night and the entire street and its adjacent roads and cul-de-sacs had come out to see her in all her fame and glory.

And when a local area is primarily made up of apartment blocks that is a lot of people trying to cram into one drag queen venue to see a current reality TV superstar who had the capacity to make social media and their hearts implode.

Across the venue, Oliver could see that the youngish man with the cap and the hair pulled over his face had returned.

Who was he?

He was noticeable because he was about the only person in there without a mask on, although his pulled forward hair certainly did a good enough job covering up what was beneath.

Wayne must have served him for he was already nursing a pint of what looked to be lager. Perhaps he would put a mask on later as many had already found that drinking and wearing a mask at the same time was far from easy; although some were achieving this with the use of straws.

Oliver didn't like the masks. They made him feel uncomfortable. Anybody could be hiding behind them. Absolutely anybody could have walked in that pub that evening with a mask on and he wouldn't have known it.

Now what was it that Wayne had said about him? His name was Jay or something that sounded like Jay. It couldn't actually be Jake, could it?

Could it be Jake... in disguise?

Idiot, what was he thinking? Of course it couldn't be Jake, in disguise or otherwise.

Jake was dead!

He had watched him slip away at the roadside. He had watched his body convulse and the blood flow thick and fast. He had watched his eyes close.

He had heard his final words of love.

I love you, Oliver. I promise I will always be with you.

He had felt his own heart splintering into a million pieces. There was never any questioning that feeling. That had been unbelievably real.

Oliver shuddered and quickly distracted himself by serving the many masked, thirsty punters that were building up at the bar who all wanted to get their drinks in before the new star of their show appeared. Wayne was thankful for the help. It was, after all, what they were both being paid to do.

Lolita Lollypop was going to help them serve shortly too, but that would be after her performance.

She had already had a crash course in pulling pints and using the till, or at least her alter ego Aaron Batts had. But in high heels and a skin-tight dress it was going to be much harder for her to bend down and retrieve bottles of alcohol from the bottom fridge shelves.

They could really do with her help now, but it was a charity night and she was giving up her time voluntarily. Maybe Martin would get stuck in but he rarely did. He was too busy playing the big I am these days or disappearing into his office for extended periods of time.

They all knew what he was probably doing in there; surfing the internet for dates or glancing through the personal columns.

Conducting business? No, not so much.

Although he was the owner, he rarely acted like it and Wayne was quickly beginning to feel as though all the responsibility of running the place was landing on his shoulders.

And his mate Robert (AKA Wendy) was no use either.

He was always too distracted being Wendy and explaining how garters and girdles worked, finding things to stuff into his bras and adding beauty spots the size of saucers to every smooth surface of skin he could find, and not always his own.

To say nothing of explaining how he had bought himself a new apron and baking tray, and had found himself with a soggy bottom and an over-sized muffin top on more than one occasion.

If the truth be known, Wayne was not happy with this current arrangement. This had once been his pub, his livelihood, his home. Now none of this was his. But sooner or later he would find his way again.

One day soon he hoped that he would have his own place again.

True, he and Robert had been friends for years and had often had many a drink and chat over the bar but this was different, that had been his bar. The roles had now shifted and he had found himself at the bottom of the pecking order.

Well, not quite at the bottom, he was just one higher than Oliver but only because he was still yet to master the fine art of changing a beer barrel.

He was particularly bothered by the fact that he had actually ended up living in

Wendy's dimly lit studio flat where they used to play poker with Digger Dave and Plumper Pete, and Robert/Wendy in turn had moved into his old living quarters above the pub.

And even after all this time living there, he was still pulling bit of Wendy's wig hair off his socks no matter how much he vacuumed the place.

But this phoenix would definitely rise from its ashes and be a success once more. He may even call his next pub The Phoenix. And there would be another pub. This was only a stop gap until then, and that was the mindset that kept him going, night after night.

This was not the end for Wayne.

Following an announcement from Martin, and as Lolita stepped into the spotlight and the audience moved towards the stage, Oliver noticed that the youngish man in the cap had not joined them but had remained sitting where he was, staring back at him across the void that had appeared as he took a large drink from his glass.

The next time Oliver looked up he was nowhere to be seen.

Maybe he had put on a mask and joined the others.

Or maybe he had left.

Q💔 CHAPTER 14 Q💔

Halloween

"Well hello there," said Lolita, stepping forward to the edge of the stage with her microphone in hand. "It's great to see so many of you here tonight inside The Queens Legs.

"Oh and hello to all those out in the street trying to peer through the windows too. They really are in the cheap seats out there, aren't they?

"You know, it's a good job so many gay men have a secret pair of high heels stashed away, just to give them that extra bit of height so they can see in. I mean let's face it; it's the only thing worth going back in the closet for, right?

"Oh and don't forget, the more you drink the more gorgeous I will become. Actually, looking at you lot, that really needs to work both ways too. Can somebody get me a drink?"

And with that she grabbed a bottle of beer from the person standing closest to her at the front of the stage and downed the contents in one before handing him back the empty bottle.

"Ha, I'm only joking, I can't see how ugly any of you are with those masks on."

Admittedly the guy she had taken the drink from should have been annoyed by this, but the amazing Miss Lolita Lollypop from 'The Black Queen' had just stolen his beer and drunk it.

He was now officially the most envied person in that building.

And what a tale there would be to tell back at work on Monday, especially when all sorts of embellishments and colourful untruths had been added to it. For by the time he had finished, everybody would think that he had had the audacity to dump her after a weekend of love and romance, and what did they think about that then, eh?

"So have you heard about Miss Camp-Isla Bacta's new boyfriend then?" asked Lolita, "he drinks too, a lot. You know I'm only joking. I love her really, warts and all, literally, warts and all. Close up, some of them are not fake, you know.

"Hey, I see that you have your very own Miss Camp-Isla Bacta here too, in the shape and form of one Miss Wendy WolfWhistle. Ahhh, let's give her a big round of applause; she is the star of your show, after all; depending who you speak to that is."

The audience gave Wendy a huge round of applause and a cheer, and one Miss WolfWhistle beamed widely and proudly at the side of the stage and waved back, ever grateful for as much attention and appreciation as she could receive.

It was, after all, her reason for living.

"Hmmm," said Lolita, winking at Wendy and then turning back to face the crowd in front of her. "I bet the last time she had a big clap, she needed antibiotics and a week off work. Only joking, Wendy! Seriously though, you need to sleep with somebody to get that. Woof woof. Oh, shut me up, please."

Other than turning off her microphone, Wendy did not know how. Still they always say any coverage has to be good coverage.

Was this good coverage?

She was being called a gonorrhea-riddled dog, after all.

Oh who cares, Lolita Lollypop said it.

"Actually, I love Wendy, isn't she fab? No, I said fab. How can she be fat when she's practically a size 'zero'; zeros are round, right? Oops, I think that's a secret. I mean I never would have known had she not told me. Oh, she's told you all that too? Okay, so not a secret then; just a big, fat, blatant lie then.

"Anyway, Wendy gate crashed my dressing room earlier asking if I would like to give her a really good roasting later on. No, wait... apologies. Not a roasting, a roast dinner.

"But do you know what; Wendy would have been a great contestant in 'The Black Queen', wouldn't she? Don't you agree that she would've been great?"

And Wendy nodded vigorously because she really would have been. And she couldn't wait to sneak back into Lolita's dressing room after her performance and tell her all about how she actually had applied for the show (which she hadn't) and how the executive producers just hadn't been able to decide between herself and Miss Anna Phylactic for a place in the house (which they hadn't) and how they had been forced to select Anna in the end because they were concerned that all the viewers would fall in love with one Miss

Wendy WolfWhistle and there wouldn't be any affection left for anybody else.

Of course, she would then go on to say how she was actually very good friends with Anna in the real world (which they weren't) because they had already competed together on a semi-professional basis at the very exclusive and much sought after Divas Beauty (drag) Queen contest.

A contest so desirable and over-subscribed, that Miss Whoopsie Daisy from 'The Black Queen' had literally been knocking down the front door to compete.

"No, honestly," continued Lolita, "what with her and Derrière La Peach in there, they could have permanently blocked out Miss Shimmy Shoo and Heaven knows with all that shoo polish on her face, she needed it.

"Anyway, whilst we are on Miss Shimmy Shoo, and believe me many have been, have you seen her about since she left the reality house? No me neither. Good, isn't it? No, I'm joking again, of course. My media training has taught me that I have to be nice about all my drag queen housemates. Not about other drag queens though, eh, Wendy?

"Okay, so what can I say about Shimmy Shoo that's nice? Hmmm, what might be something nice to say about Shimmy? Oh I know... No, wait, I can't say that... I really can't say that... And I shouldn't say that, but I might... What? You already know.

"Oh yes, I know. Well, Shimmy is a real honey. No, not honey, that's not the word I'm looking for. Oh yes, that's it... the bitch is a real hunty. And don't you dare tell her I said that because I don't want her getting in contact with me.

"So, I hear Instagram is drowning in photos of her with all these celebrities who just can't get enough of her. I also hear that she was spotted recently in *Madam Tussauds* taking loads of selfies. You work it out, you look a clever bunch, but that might just be the masks.

"Okay, let's park Shimmy for a while because the way she is saturating her market, she'll be off the road in no time anyway. And whilst talking about write-offs, let's move onto my gorgeous, drag queen mother Miss Derrière La Peach.

"So, I presume you all remember the old banger from 'The Black Queen'? A steady drip from the front; toxic gas coming out the back; unlikely to ever make a sale no matter how many fresh coats of paint you put on it?

"Oops sorry, I may have reverted back to Shimmy again then. Ha, only joking. Hey, I have to be nice about her, don't I? As it seems that in a recent survey held by writer Tobias International, more people loved her than loved me in the house, but that's okay because she really was great in there, wasn't she?

"However, I must remind you that people used to love cigarettes. They even used to think smoking was good for you and look how that turned out? Hey, I'm just saying. You can interpret that how you want. I'm not saying she's bad for anyone's health.

"Okay, I'm going to sing you a few songs now and again the more you drink, the better I will sound, so drink up. You know, just like you do when you're listening to Shimmy's debut album.

"Oh somebody stop me, please."

Halloween

And so after the show, when Lolita was in her dressing room freshening up before she went out to help them on the bar, there was a knock on the door and Wendy came barging in without even an invitation to enter.

"Oh my God," she exclaimed to Lolita, excitedly sitting herself down so close to her that the reality TV star was almost poked in the face by Wendy's cheap, false eyelashes. "You were so good tonight."

"Ahhh, thank you, Darling. And will I see you on stage tonight too?"

"Oh yes, I have a few little tricks up my sleeve too. I will be doing my rendition of the *Dying Swan* again. You see what it is, is I pop on this gorgeous, teeny tiny little wedding dress that used to belong to another really famous TV reality star with huge boobie doopers that gets married a lot and I die on stage. It's all such a crowd pleaser."

"And do you die on stage often?" asked Lolita, before picking up her lipstick and quickly re-applying.

"Only during that act," replied Wendy, memorising exactly how Lolita applied her makeup for future use.

"It sounds great," replied Lolita, putting down her lipstick which Wendy would probably try and steal later when Lolita was not looking or helping out on the bar.

For if she was wearing Lolita's lipstick and she was in drag and applying it exactly the same way as Lolita did, surely that would make her Lolita... or at the very least a single, white drag queen with a history of delusion.

"Right, well, I'm off to serve behind the bar with Wayne and that little cutie I briefly met earlier. What's his name again? Oliver, is it?"

"Yes, but first of all," announced Wendy, taking very little notice of anything Lolita was saying "and just like Shimmy does when she's out and about, see I was listening to you, I would love to take some selfies too with a celebrity."

Lolita was just about to ask Wendy if she was implying that she looked imitation, but never had a chance because Wendy was on her and all around her snapping away on her camera phone, every which way but up.

"Oooh lovely," declared Wendy, quickly showing them to her afterwards. "Stunning. Gorgeous. What a treat to be photographed with such a divine and amazing drag queen talent."

"Thanks Darling."

"You're very welcome."

Wendy thought she had better say something nice about Lolita too, but she couldn't think of a single thing to say. She had already complemented her performance, what else was there to say? She, Wendy, was after all the star of the show in this venue.

"If I friend request you on social media, will you accept?" she finally said. "Then I can tag you into all my posts."

"Hmmm, well, I guess so," replied Lolita, reluctantly though as she wasn't looking for yet another online stalker.

"Do it now," demanded Wendy, quickly flicking through various pages on her mobile phone and clicking certain parts of the screen. "And then I can share all these lovely photos with you."

"What?"

"Get your phone out now and accept me. I've already sent you a friend request. How exciting for us both; best friends forever. I bet you can't wait."

Even more reluctantly than before although she had the charisma to fake smile throughout the entire process of doing it, Lolita took out her phone and accepted Wendy's friend request.

She could always change her mind in a few days time when the friendship had already turned cold and she was miles away in the comfort and safety of her own home and Wendy was nowhere nearby to bug her to accept her friend request again.

For Cyberspace was notorious for accidentally deleting friends on social media.

It happened to Wendy all the time!

But by then it would be too late for a few days would have passed and the photos and the messages and the social media tags would have been published for the entire world to see. And by then, it would be too late to change the twisted hands of fate.

It would be out there and it would be seen and it would contribute to the worst possible outcome for somebody.

***

The Queen of Hearts.

The Queen of Cups.

Divinatory meaning: Honesty and devotion, pleasure, happiness and success.

If reversed: Dishonour, displeasure and unhappiness.

Maybe even a broken heart.

Maybe even something much worse than that.

After all, a broken heart can be mended.

A broken life is a completely different story altogether.

Q❤ CHAPTER 16 Q❤

Back to late October

They would come for him.

Sooner or later, they would hunt him down just so they could seek him out and then he would be a part of it too.

But not just him, they wanted everybody who was in there to be a part of it. Nobody was safe; everybody was accountable.

No exceptions.

And all around his agitated and tired head the bells rang relentlessly, just like they had done that night at Divas cabaret bar, and again, like then, he had no control over any of it.

Underneath his bunk bed, pressed up as close as he could against the wall, Chris tried to put his hands over his ears to block out as much of the noise as he could, but he couldn't block it out. Nor could he block out the fact that they were coming for him and they would make him a part of this.

Whether he wanted to be involved or not, they would drag him into it and they would make him accountable just for being there. 'United as one' they would shout.

But this was not even close to what he wanted; for he had his own plans and it did not include this or what anybody else wanted or expected of him. He was finally taking control of his own life again and this was a severe breech of his own destiny.

It sounded as though prison cells around him were being ransacked, followed by cheers and roars from fellow prisoners.

Images from films and television programmes constantly shot through his mind; every bang was followed by a scream; every scream could be followed by a river of blood.

And he could be the next in line to fall.

Shortly his cell would be ransacked and if he didn't move and quickly hide somewhere else he too could be buried under the remaining devastation of the prison riots.

He was no longer safe in his cell. He knew he had no other choice but to move to a safer location, if such a thing even existed.

God only know where this started or where the prison officers were or what was really happening on the other side of his cell door.

Where was 'Moustache'? Was he safe? Did Chris really care? This had become a dog eat dog environment and his own safety was paramount.

He slipped out from under his hiding place and looked quickly around at the few items he owned in there. There was nothing of any value that he needed to take with him. There was certainly nothing that he needed to destroy before anybody else could get their grubby hands on it.

He put his ear to the door, but it made very little difference; the noise of the riots could be heard from every direction.

He just needed to get out of there and into the corridors. He just needed to find somewhere else to hide until this was all over. Although that may not be as easy as he hoped. After all, the access doors would all be locked, wouldn't they?

He hadn't fully prepared himself for what he expected to see out in the corridors; it was without a doubt much worse than he had anticipated. There was mess everywhere; including the contents of other cells and several bodies lay unconscious on the floor.

People were running in every direction or tripping up and falling over things that had previously had a safe place to live.

Someone ran into him as they charged past. He was in their way and he fell hard against the brick wall. He banged his head and scraped his hand as he tried to support himself, but apart from a few scratches and some short, sharp immediate pain he was fine. He continued along the corridor but there was very little escape from what was going on around him.

Seriously, where were the prison officers? They were nowhere to be seen. Whoever had mastered this plan had meticulously covered every detail.

He turned a corner where he expected the access door to be locked, but it was wide open, as was the next one and the one after that too.

He kept running, faster and faster, caring less and less as he pushed and shoved the slower ones out of the way. He had had it done to him, now that was the precedence. All he cared about was his own safety and looking after himself. He had no friends in there, he didn't owe anybody anything. It was him against them all.

It was always him against them all.

Surely the riot police or equivalent must be on their way? The prisoners wouldn't be allowed to run riot forever. Somebody somewhere would have to stop them soon. Hopefully they were already on their way. The authorities must know what was happening by now.

His cell had probably been destroyed by this time. Thankfully he wasn't in there. Fleeing from his hiding place had been a good decision, hopefully the first of many to come.

Now where would be safe to hide until then; inside or outside?

Outside would be safer, but was that even an option?

All the access doors within the building seemed to be open, he had yet to find one that he hadn't been able to make his way through, maybe there was one open that led out to the recreational space.

Yes, outside was a good decision.

He changed direction. He wasn't too far away from where he needed to be. He ran quickly and solidly where he could. Other times he scrambled over broken furniture, mattresses and unconscious or hurt bodies.

He was not one of them and that was all he could focus on. He would not be made accountable for any of this. None of this was down to him. This would not show on his record.

And that too was a good decision.

Now what else?

He found a door that led to the outside recreational space and pushed it hard and it opened, pretty much as he expected it too. He ran outside and into the clear, clean air and it instantly felt safer out there. It was certainly calmer, but for how long?

He was very surprised to see that nobody else was out there. Even more surprised that nobody else had made such a good decision as he had.

Then he saw why there was possibly nobody else out there and he had another decision to make.

There in front of him was the opportunity he had been waiting for.

There in front of him was an open door that would lead him right out of there.

The door to his freedom.

Suddenly, everything changed. Different sirens began to roar around the high walls of the complex. Action was finally being taken to stop all of this. They would swoop around the building and attack from the outside in. The world was taking control again. The riots would soon be over.

The atmosphere instantly changed and momentarily so did his chain of thought.

But the door to his freedom remained open.

However, this was a limited opportunity. It wouldn't be available for much longer, perhaps just a matter of seconds, if that.

He walked ever closer to it, knowing that time was no longer on his side.

It was now or never.

His freedom was calling him.

It was his for the taking.

The door to his freedom.

Time was really running out.

He continued to walk forward, quicker and quicker.

The door to his freedom.

The door to his past.

The door to his present.

The door to his future.

It was the door to his freedom.

He could hide on the outside; maybe even in disguise.

Yes, it was all his for the taking.

And now... a short intermission

"Hi there, I'm Miss Shimmy Shoo and you probably best know me from starring in 'The Black Queen'.

"Today I am going to tell you all about my fabulicious, brand new autobiography *'If the Shoo fits wear it'*.

"It's exciting, it's daring and it's very, very sexy. Four hundred pages all about me, can you imagine anything else more sublime?

"Want to know if all those gossip columns are correct, then you're going to have to buy my book and find out.

"*If the Shoo fits wear it* by me Miss Shimmy Shoo is available in participating retailers now, whilst stocks last.

"Remember, a book in the hand, is worth two in my bush."

Forward to early November

April Showers, but as a man, was relaxing at home when he was disturbed by an unexpected and somewhat startling discovery.

Actually, he was relaxing in a lovely bubble bath when he saw it.

He had literally just let some of the water out and had topped up with some more hot after having shaved off a few stray hairs that had dared to present themselves on his manly chin before 'The Black Queen' star needed to drag himself up to grace the red carpet at a film premiere that very evening.

Yes, life was good for April since leaving the reality TV house. He was enjoying the fame that it had brought although he was not milking it as much as some of the others had done or still were (i.e. one Miss Shimmy Shoo who seemed to insist on being on everything).

April's psychic days now most definitely seemed to be a thing of the past particularly since appearing in the reality TV show; with the consensus very much being in favour of her having been a fake all along in that regard.

However, when in drag, most viewers had actually believed that she was a woman disguised as a drag queen and had entered the house under false pretence; little did they know, of course.

A belief that had quickly escalated and had granted her the title of 'Britain's fishiest drag queen' which naturally Shimmy Shoo despised and often protested against to anybody who would listen or write down in a published article. After all, she was much fishier than April in so many ways and in better ways too.

In fact, Shimmy was so much fishier in comparison to April and in so many ways that she actually reeked of it.

And just for the record, Shimmy hadn't actually said that, but Lolita Lollypop once did on a national TV chat show before being made to retract it by Shimmy's legal representatives.

So April had shaved the rogue chin hairs, had topped up the hot water and was now relaxing in the bath before the events of the evening beckoned him in full drag alongside one's very best dress, accessories, hair and makeup; not forgetting the trademark hourglass figure either.

Which incidentally, if it had been real, would not have fitted into the bathtub and April would have been in the shower instead and the unexpected and startling discovery may not have been made.

Perhaps then, the terrible event that followed would most certainly have been avoided.

If only he had foreseen the possibilities before reaching for his mobile phone whilst relaxing in the bath that day.

If only he had been able to switch on April's psychic powers and foresee what was coming.

But he didn't know what this would result in and he reached for his phone and innocently searched through social media to see what was happening in the world.

He always ignored the articles about himself.

He really didn't care what people wrote or said about Miss April Showers and he particularly paid no attention to the unflattering hash tags or the snidely remarks made by people who were not fans or had taken it upon themselves to hate her, stalk her or troll her on social media.

He did like to look at some of their profiles though and was amused to discover that social media trolls actually were just that in every sense of the word. What with their piggy little screwed-up faces, podgy noses, mean little eyes and bad hair, they really were just like trolls in every sense of the word.

It would probably also explain why they were being abusive about her and not out with their friends, especially on a weekend evening.

So, just because he didn't look at April's insults, it didn't mean that he didn't look at others. Camp-Isla Bacta and Shimmy seemed to be the worst recipients of the negative feedback, but it was always slightly fun to see what feedback the others were also receiving from the public.

Apart from issues about her weight, Derrière La Peach tended to fare quite well.

Lolita had a mixed bag of feedback; some good, some bad, some indifferent.

Robyn RedBreasts however had been missing from social media for a while and her feedback was starting to drop off. After all, if she was not going to respond or tell the paparazzi how upsetting she found it all then there was no fun in posting anything; at least that's how the whole thing seemed to work.

April started flicking through Lolita's comments. Lots of positives about her tour, that was good. A number of I love Lolita's. A number of I hate Lolita's too.

Oh well, you can't please everyone.

Oh, what was this? Some photos... Photos of Lolita and some rancid, old drag queen who looked like she had just climbed out of a landfill site.

Wait a minute, I recognise her...

Was she...?

Could she be the one who...?

Oh my God, she was the one who called me a fraud when I was the Psychic Drag Queen.

Now what was her name again?

Oh, she couldn't remember it then and she still couldn't remember it now.

Yes, it was definitely her.

She read the caption carefully and studied the photos intently.

'Me and my best new gal-pal #Lolitalollypop at #TheQueensLegspub. I look better in drag tho.'

April shook her head, for she really didn't look better than her in drag at all!

Without a moment's hesitation, she called a number on speed dial. "Lolita, hi, it's April here. How are you? ... Good. Listen can you do me a favour? I'm looking at some pictures of you recently at a pub called The Queen's Legs with what I can only describe to be Britain's ugliest drag queen. Who is she? ... Wendy WolfWhistle, okay that's not quite the name I thought you were going to say, but it sounds familiar now ... Oh, I don't know how about Ronda the Rancid. So where is this place then? ... Thanks, oh and on East Green Street did you say? Okay, looks like I'll be paying a little visit to this East Green Street at some point. See you later, cheers then."

And with that, he put down his phone, drained away the contents of the bath and started the process of transforming himself into one Miss April Showers for the evening ahead.

Wendy and this East Green Street would have to wait for the moment.

But they wouldn't wait for long.

Q💔 CHAPTER 18 Q💔

Early November

Tequila was performing on the stage.

It was a very sexy, erotic number that Martin had not wanted her to do, but she knew the fans would love it and she knew she would love performing it to them.

Her inner whore was begging to be unleashed.

And it gave her the perfect opportunity to wear the skimpiest outfit she could to show off her gorgeous, perfect little figure.

♫ I'm waiting in the dark room
You'll find everything you need by touch alone
When I'm waiting in the dark room
I can be there on my own
But it's better when there are two
But only me and you

Step inside
Leave your inhibitions at the door
Come inside
You'll be begging me for more
It's never gonna stop
It's never ever gonna stop

Could you want me in a dark room?
Could you love me in a dark room?
You can be anyone you want to be
Your secrets are safe with me ♫

Not all secrets were safe though; especially not with her!

But Tequila had a secret too and so far it had stayed very safe as she was the only one who knew about it.

And Tequila had never told anybody about her secret because she didn't think anybody would have believed her.

And why would they believe her? It was quite absurd; especially when she barely even believed it herself.

♫ *I'm waiting in the dark room*
It's so quiet I can almost hear you breathe
When I'm waiting in the dark room
There's only me and you
And it's better when there are two
But only me and you

Step my way
Can you hear me call your name?
I'm over here
Things will never be the same
Now that you're here
You'll never want to leave
You'll never ever want to leave

Could you want me in a dark room?
Could you love me in a dark room?
You can be anyone you want to be
Your secrets are safe with me ♫

Tequila had debated sharing this secret, time and time again, but who would she tell?

Was it even a secret or was she just withholding some unknown facts that may not even be the truth?

The more she thought about it, the more real it now seemed.

Or was it?

She wasn't sure again.

♫ *We're meeting in the dark room*
Should I let you in?

We're meeting in the dark room
Let the hunger games begin

Could you want me in a dark room?
Could you love me in a dark room?
You can be anyone you want to be
Your secrets are safe with me

Your secrets are safe with me...
For now ♫

She hadn't really thought about it much for quite a while, but recent discoveries had refreshed the memory.

She had thought about it a lot when she was recovering in hospital, but as the weeks passed by and as she was preparing the cabaret show, perfecting dance routines, and trying to keep Wendy out of anything backless, crotchless or legless, it fell out of her head.

But now it was back.

And it was firmly back; rooted in; unmoveable; clinging tightly like a limpet on a rock.

That night...

That blasted night when Divas had burnt down, she had seen him too.

Or at least she thought she had.

Wendy had resuscitated her and as she came around, she thought she had seen Jake too.

He was in the distance, away from everybody else but it certainly looked like him from where she was.

But she had just come around and everything was unclear.

But it is very difficult, if not near on impossible, to un-see something once it has been seen.

But if it wasn't him, then what was it?

Q❦ CHAPTER 19 Q❦

Early November

Wendy was quietly sitting at her makeup mirror in her dressing room, tucked behind the stage at The Queen's Legs cabaret bar.

As she generously applied the first undercoat of fluorescent beige to her porous man skin in preparation for the evening shows ahead, she couldn't help but smile at how wonderful life was now that she was in the show.

In her head, she was acting out her scenes, over and over again. Each time improving upon her last performance and daring to be the best. Like a true professional, she demanded the entire spotlight and she would not be satisfied until she had absorbed every little bit of it.

For that reason, she hadn't initially noticed the envelope that had been sitting there so patiently staring up at her.

Perhaps she was also too pre-occupied by her own stunning beauty or maybe she was over-whelmed by the new figure-hugging leggings that Tequila had just dropped off for her to wear whilst lip-syncing to a *Grease* medley which she could just about get one leg into and had almost pulled up to the voluptuous curves of her giant man arse.

But there it was, sitting on the dressing table staring back at her, an envelope addressed to her with her name on it; Miss Wendy WolfWhistle, written in beautiful handwriting, propped up against the vase of plastic flowers that she had recently bought herself (but claimed were from a fan) and sprayed with air freshener every couple of days for a more realistic aroma.

Whatever could it be?

Possibly, it was a letter from a fan that was madly in love with her? How very exciting and about time too.

She instantly put down the washing up sponge that she had been using to colour in her face with, always being careful not to use the green scratchy side, and eagerly tore it open, with little bits of envelope flying in every direction.

Was it a fan letter? It had to be, why else would it be in her presence waiting for her tiny, agile, well-manicured fingers to pop it open?

It was, it was, it really was a fan letter and this time it was from a real person and not something she had created herself and then purposefully left beside the beer pumps at the bar in mass volume, for people to find and return to her.

"Ooh for me?" she would often exclaim when one of them was handed back to her. "How wonderful, I wonder who it is from? An extremely grateful fan I expect or a lover of my work, no doubt."

But everybody always knew who they were from. Especially as they tended to have beetroot stains on the envelope and beer soaking through them and they always tended to say exactly the same thing.

And why wouldn't they say the same thing? It's not like the photocopier at the library was going to change even a single word. Pity really because it needed to.

'Wendy your gresat and soooo pretty to! ♥'

'Love you Wendy, your brill and dead talented.'

'Can't weight to see you're next show Wendy. Do a pelvic frust just for me, yeah xx'

But this time it was genuine and it was thoughtful and it was charming and there was not a spelling mistake anywhere, not that she probably would have been able to spot one anyway.

She was loved, really and truly and somebody had taken the time to tell her how wonderful she was.

She would have to tell Martin all about this immediately. Oooh, how jealous he would be when he read it for he never ever received any attention at all whilst she literally drowned in it.

And it didn't matter that her face was only partially covered. And it didn't matter that she was virtually naked bar from an unstuffed bra, a pair of Granny knickers that she had not yet tucked herself into properly, and it certainly didn't matter that her armpits were so hairy that monkeys could swing very happily from them.

The important thing is that she had been sent a fan letter and she needed to tell somebody immediately.

And telling somebody, anybody, just one person, was of course the start of the journey to telling everybody.

She found Martin quietly sitting and reading the paper when she charged into his office like a bull in a china shop or a drag queen at a sequin or bobbin sale, shrieking her delight at having received such a heart-warming piece of literature.

He put down his paper and took the letter from Wendy. He would always claim, if asked, that he was keeping afloat of current affairs which was very important for a business man to do, but the 'Men seeking Men' page in the local periodical more than often led to a different type of current affair.

"Wendy," he eventually exclaimed, after he had carefully read it through twice.

"I know," she proudly responded, "hopefully the first of many more to come."

"I hope for your sake it isn't," he replied, with a twist of concern in his voice.

"Why would you say that? It's a fan letter. Don't you want me to be adored?"

"Wendy, this is hate mail. Your fan didn't send this."

"It's not hate mail at all; you're clearly reading it wrong. Look, just give it back. I'm sorry I showed it to you now."

"Wendy, this isn't good. Seriously, you need to take this straight to the police." He could tell that she had stopped listening because he wasn't saying anything that she wanted to hear. "Wendy, listen to me, somebody is threatening you."

"No, they are not. It's delicious and divine, just like the new eight pounds wig I am going to grace the boards with tonight."

"So you don't think: 'You are so bad and you make me sick' and 'you need to be killed' are anything to worry about?"

"Martin, that's how people talk these days," she stupidly replied. "You need to get with the times. Bad and sick are good and if you kill something then you are great at it. Just ask Tequila."

"People may talk like that, but they don't normally put it into a letter using cut and paste words from different magazines. Wendy, this is really serious."

"No, you're wrong, give me back my fan letter and I will finish getting ready. I don't want you breathing your jealousy over it any longer."

Martin reluctantly handed it back to her and watched her leave the room. What with so much sag in her Granny knickers and her lower back hair tucked into them, it was not a pleasant sight to behold.

Had he interpreted the letter incorrectly? He didn't think he had. Okay, Wendy might have had a point, but seriously how could: 'It looks like your face has exploded when you drag up' mean anything else other than what those carefully cut out and pasted words said.

Hmmm, there had been some truth in what had been written though, after all.

He returned to his paper, trying hard to focus on the literary content of something more important.

Middle aged man with a nagging wife and more kids than he can count, looking for fun with similar aged man or younger. 'Local celebrity' drag queens with wonky boobs need not re-apply, irrespective of how much weight you think you have lost.

Martin marked a circle around that one.

Nobody ever said the path to true love would be a smooth one.

Mark (AKA Connie) sat underneath the warm autumn sun on his usual bench staring out towards the sea as he unpacked his picnic lunch.

This really was the life, free from one and all and everything.

As he sat, slowly munching on a peanut butter sandwich which he had most afternoons, his mind wandered back to the early summer, to Divas, to the drugs, to his previous existence, to the fire, and in particular to the very evil Chris Randall.

How he hated that man and nobody had ever destroyed a life as much as he had.

Mark was grateful every single day that he was no longer a part of his life.

But that afternoon he was unable to shake off the past in the way that he normally did. And for once he was particularly focusing on a specific time in his recent past where he had arrived late for the cabaret show at Divas, and Tittie and Tequila had had to help drag him up in just a matter of minutes.

God knows he had even had to go out onto the stage with his false eyelashes falling off; as he recalled resembling windscreen wipers across his face.

Tittie had asked Mark where he had been, but he had not responded. Tittie knew better than to push it but probably presumed that he was with some god-awful client somewhere obtaining drug money by the hour.

However, the truth is that Mark hadn't wanted anybody to know where he had been that day and it certainly hadn't been where he thought they would presume it was.

But sometimes in life, it was easier just to let people think what they wanted to think and to let them believe it. It helped eliminate any awkward questions for he had been in negotiations with The Maniac.

For one never spoke of The Maniac. He was a bad man, a very bad man who made Chris Randall look like the cutest kitten in comparison.

The deal with him had been a hard one to agree and it had taken a lot longer than he had anticipated but it had led to his freedom, even if it meant that others had been caught up in the backlash along the way.

Especially Tequila, but Tequila was not aware of that.

His dealings with The Maniac had led him to this day, to the day before and the day before that too. It had led to him being able to sit and eat sandwiches on the promenade, every afternoon, if he wanted to. To breathe in the fresh air and live a life without retribution and mostly with sobriety.

It had also led Chris to his current existence.

Mark had ended up dominating Chris. He had had to live and abide by the Law of Connie Lingus or Licious as she later became known when Chris made her the star of the show. Something he was very much not supportive of but had absolutely no control over at all.

Mark had held all the cards back then and now he held none. He didn't need to; he had no use for them. But sometimes a card is unexpectedly dealt, and all you can do is stick, or twist and hope for a better hand.

But that particular afternoon, Mark could not clear his mind. The past had worked its way into his mind a few times before but he had always been able to suppress it, but for some reason on this afternoon he couldn't push it away. It wouldn't go away. It just stayed there, parked like a bad smell in a confined space, without any ventilation to release the demon. And he didn't like feeling this way at all.

If it hadn't been for his previous existence, the deal that broke Chris would not have been made. Living life on the edge in such a manner as he once did then the people you meet are similar, like minded, greedy and obnoxiously vile.

But so long as he did most of it as Connie, it wasn't really him doing it. Sometimes he had to do it as Mark and he didn't like that as much, but it depended on the situation, but Connie was always the scapegoat and the preferred option for him.

Those birds of a feather really flocked together and Chris was really set up through those new contacts that appeared like an oasis on the pavements of despair.

It had not taken much persuasion from Mark for Chris to change his plans, particularly if he felt he was getting something better out of it.

Particularly, if he had no reason to doubt his own cousin.

Particularly, if he believed he could be rich beyond his wildest dreams.

Particularly, if all Connie had requested was to be the star of the cabaret show in return for such a massive financial lifeline.

That was a very small price to pay in comparison to the much bigger gain, wasn't it?

Maybe this is what was meant as fool's gold.

Divas cabaret bar was flagging, it had been for ages. The show was tired, the punters had grown bored and his debts were escalating out of control. The new deal had sorted that for him too, in the short-term at least, but the benefits were not reaped quickly enough.

The rewards were limited and the Heavies were heavier than he had ever experienced before. They kept changing the stakes, making more demands, pushing the barriers.

Chris had been unable to control the situation. He needed to flee, to be safe but he had nowhere to run. And the ongoing battle of his unrequited love for Oliver had only confused the situation even more.

Little did he know that his own cousin was the ring leader and was personally hand delivering him to the chair that was about to execute him.

Little did he know that this was payback for the years of abuse Mark had endured from him.

Little did he know that sometimes the demands that came back were not from The Maniac; sometimes, Mark just did it for his own entertainment.

Little did he know that more than often Mark pocketed the repayments himself and then advised that Chris was unable to make his payment that day.

But ultimately, little did Chris know that the fire and his prison cell would give him the greatest freedom of all.

However, this was only half the story and Mark was in a lot deeper than he initially anticipated he ever would be.

He put down his half-eaten sandwich and succumbed to his emotions. He knew this was going to happen. He had sensed it looming in the very depths of his inner self.

He didn't want to go back, but his past was pleading for him to return. He always feared it would, but now the emotions were too strong to ignore anymore. Guilt and regret were burrowing deep within him and there was no way out.

He never wanted to go back. Not to that god-forsaken town with all its history and eccentricities but he was no longer able to fight the demands of his own guilt any longer.

He would have to return.

He would once more have to walk along the tired streets of that tired town; hidden once more by the shadows of the night. Hoping and praying that nobody would spot him, or judge him or know anything about him as he attempted to remain unseen by the eyes of anybody who once used to know this local boy.

Damn it, he had to return there. There was no other choice.

He wouldn't be able to live with himself if he didn't. He had to right the wrongs that he had made along the way.

The last time, his actions had almost killed Miss Tequila ShockingBird, and Wendy had had to save her life.

This time, he was the only one who would be able to save Tequila's life.

Forward to 5ᵗʰ November - Bonfire night

The bonfire night fireworks were about to begin and the punters began to wander eagerly to the pub's exit and out onto East Green Street to see them. Not one person wanted to miss a single bang or explosion.

Wayne turned to Oliver who was enviously watching them all go outside, for he wanted to be out there too watching the display. "Could you change the lager barrel for me? It would be a good time now whilst it's quiet."

Oliver looked reluctantly back at him. He had tried several times to master the art of changing a barrel, but had so far not been able to; too many pipes and things to turn and take off and not enough time to put everything back into place.

It would be so much easier and so much quicker if everybody just drunk from bottles or if Wayne changed the barrel instead.

"Go on, you'll be fine," said Wayne trying to reassure him. "Look, if you find that you really can't do it then I will do it, but you must at least try."

Oliver made no attempt to hide that he really didn't want to, but it was part of his job and Wayne was his supervisor. Plus, he really hated going down into those deep, dark cellars that spread out underneath the world outside.

They were vast and eerie and the situation was not helped in anyway by the flickering, low-voltage bulbs that barely let out any light at all, to say nothing of the overpowering stench of damp down there and the constant sensation of scuttling, just out of sight.

Maybe he should just quit instead, but was it really worth giving up his job because he couldn't change a barrel or even be bothered to learn how to do it or that Wayne always seemed to boss him around or he didn't like going into the cellars?

It probably wasn't, but somehow he just hadn't been able to stop thinking about it that night. Agreeing to work there probably was a mistake in hindsight, but was it the worst mistake he had ever made? Probably not, but he did want to leave.

His life had been without fun and laughter for what seemed like such a long time now and he needed to take that first step to improving his own wellbeing. This job was actually delaying that now. All he ever seemed to do was work.

Oliver walked past the dwindling crowd that was still flocking outside to watch the fireworks and headed for the door next to the toilets which led the way down to the cellar.

As he stood there briefly contemplating the bleakness below, the toilet door opened and Jay, or the one he was referring to as Jay, walked through and stepped back into the pub and their eyes momentarily met. Oliver looked away immediately.

He pushed open the cellar door firmly and then stepped inside, the door closing slowly behind him as he walked carefully down the old stone steps, holding onto the rickety, old handrail and taking great care not to fall.

He really hated it down there.

Of course, he didn't actually need to be working there and in hindsight why was he?

He knew that Wendy and Martin had both been so good to him and was it unfair to let them down, especially during the first few weeks of their grand opening?

But did he care enough to stay?

Could he leave them high and dry?

But his own wellbeing had to be his first priority.

Maybe a strange person who kept coming in and staring at him and then disappearing could be more than enough of a reason to leave?

Behind him, just as he reached the cold, concrete floor below, the door at the top of the stone steps finally closed into its wooden frame. He shuddered slightly as though somebody had just walked right through him, but that was probably just the chill of the air down there. At least he hoped it was.

He walked over to the barrels and examined them closely. Right this one is lager, this one is not. Is this the empty one or is it this one?

He turned around in a panic. He had had heard a noise....

What the Hell was that?

Was somebody down there with him?

He could feel his heart beating through his chest.

He heard the noise again; louder this time.

Oh, it's the bloody fireworks outside. Thank God for that.

This place really scared the crap out of him.

Okay, so you're a lager barrel and you're probably something else. So then what are you?

Hmmm, can I seriously be arsed with this? At worst if I manage to make this work, cider will probably flow through the lager pump. At best, Wayne will have to change the lager himself.

That really would be the easiest option.

Actually, resigning would be the easiest option.

Suddenly, Oliver knew what he had to do.

**

It would be a while before anybody realised that Oliver had gone. His absence would only be noted once the fireworks were over and the queues had once more built up at the bar.

Martin would ask where Oliver was and Wayne would explain that he was changing a barrel but now thinking about it, actually that was ages ago.

Martin would check the cellar but he would not be able to see Oliver down there.

And the barrel would still need changing.

So then what on Earth had happened to Oliver?

Had he left them high and dry after all; just as he thought he might?

And what had become of Jay or the one that Oliver thought might be called Jay?

That evening, unlike the others, Jay did not leave early. He sat on a seat opposite the bar and nursed his pint until closing time.

Just sitting there and watching there and waiting there.

But waiting there for what?

The day after Bonfire night

The next morning, just as they were about to open, Martin was looking around his bar.

It seemed as though something wasn't quite right, but what? Had things been moved, and if they had, what had moved?

Something just felt slightly different than it had when he had locked up the evening before.

A used glass sat on the bar which he felt certain hadn't been there before.

Everything was always tidied up and put away before he retired for the night, he was insistent upon that. His staff would know that. They wouldn't leave a dirty glass out for the morning shift to tidy up.

The cardboard holder that the nuts were attached to was no longer hanging on the wall. It now lay flat on the bar shelf that ran across the fridges adjacent to all the bottles of spirits.

He went to hang it back up but the packaging was torn and it no longer hung where it should. It seemed as though some of the nuts were missing too.

One of the stools that ran along the bar was also slightly misaligned in comparison to the others. He was not OCD or anal, or at least he didn't think he was, he was just very proud of the establishment and whilst everything was shiny and new, he wanted it all arranging in a certain way. He just wanted it to be the best it could be.

Everything else looked as though it was in place; exactly as it had looked the evening before when he had gone upstairs after a long evening shift. Nothing else looked as though it had moved; except for those few things.

Maybe Wendy had come down for a midnight snack... again.

He would have to tell her off about that... again.

***

Shortly afterwards, perhaps a little later than lunchtime, Oliver's Mother entered The Queen's Legs. Her poker face gave nothing away which could in itself indicate that she was not happy about something.

She headed straight towards the bar where Wayne, Robert (AKA Wendy) and Martin stood chatting. She looked at each one in turn. There really was no mistaking Wendy WolfWhistle as a man, drag queen or otherwise; irrespective of what was reflected back from the mirror that she used to drag herself up in.

Around the venue sat love struck couples having a drink together or maybe planning to move in together after just three dates because this time they had definitely found 'the one'.

Groups of friends were also catching up on their day off and a couple of lonely men perhaps waiting for an unexpected twist of luck to come their way sat by themselves.

She couldn't help but wonder if that was how Oliver was perceived when he had first arrived in town when nobody knew him.

"What can I get you, Love?" asked Wayne.

"Oh, I'm not here for a drink," she replied. "I am worried about my son Oliver. I believe he works here."

"Well, he did," butted in Martin but he walked out last night without any reason why. In fact he didn't even say anything to anybody."

"Oh dear," replied Oliver's Mother. "I am sorry to hear that and you haven't heard from him at all today?"

"No."

"Oh, I was hoping to catch him in here."

"You could try his flat," suggested Robert, "it's just down the road. Do you have his address?"

"I have been there already, he's not in," she replied. "That's why I came here. Oh I knew something was wrong. You see, it's my birthday today and we were supposed to be meeting a while ago for lunch. He hasn't even phoned me or anything. Not even as much as a text message from him. This is so not like him. So not like him at all."

"Happy birthday," said a different voice to the side of her.

She turned and noticed a young man holding forth his pint in fair cheer. She hadn't noticed him standing there before. He was wearing a cap and his hair was pushed over his face. It was Jay and he had been in there drinking since they had opened.

She smiled politely at him and quickly thanked him for the birthday wishes, even though she really had no idea who she was speaking to.

She thanked the men for the information and then left the pub, none the wiser and even more concerned than she had been beforehand.

Jay put down his unfinished drink and followed her out and watched her walk down the street.

***

An hour or so later, Oliver's Mother received a short text message from him wishing her a happy birthday and apologising for forgetting about their lunch date.

The message, compared to his usual correspondence, was short and slightly abrupt but perhaps understandable in his current state of mind.

But Oliver's Mother knew that something was wrong; terribly, terribly wrong.

Somebody was using his mobile phone.

For she had not made any plans to meet him for lunch.

And that day was not her birthday.

The day after Bonfire night

Mark (AKA Connie) stood outside Divas Cabaret Bar, pretty much as Oliver had done just a few days previously and took in the view of devastation, heart ache and reconstruction.

This had all been his doing.

Well, him and The Maniac.

It was being done up, a business was investing money in the shell, lovingly breathing life back into it.

Yes, like it needed to in all of them, the phoenix would rise once more.

He looked around before making his way from there. Nothing else seemed to have changed.

He had not planned on standing there for long, he had no emotional attachment, and in fact he felt more disappointed that there was actually still something to see there. He had rather hoped that there would just be a big hole in the ground; a huge gap between the neighbouring buildings.

Now parts of the previous building would continue on within the new. The building would never be quite dead. It would live on in whatever it went on to become.

The building was really of no interest to Mark, it had just been a small detour from the train station. He had lived in this town all his life and he knew it would only take a few minutes out of his day to get there.

He knew that town so well. He knew how it looked in the sun or the rain; he knew how it looked in the light and in the darkness, especially the darkness.

Had he returned home? It didn't feel like home, not anymore. If anything it just felt like that place where he used to exist.

He instantly felt suffocated.

This was definitely not his town, not anymore. He was no longer a resident there, nor was he a local, but he could be and he would be perceived by many as that.

He shared the same local knowledge as they did and this town was listed as his place of birth on his passport.

But as he walked from one street to another, remembering, trying not to remember, regretting, not regretting, sighing or sometimes smiling just a little bit because it hadn't all been bad, he felt that he still belonged there.

But he didn't want to belong there.

And even when he checked into his hotel, which was near enough to the train station in case he needed to make a quick escape but still far enough to hide away in, he was asked if he was from around here.

They said there was something familiar about the way he spoke. His accent was a local one.

He had only been recognised by his voice alone. In hindsight that might not necessarily be a bad thing, it might mean he could blend in more.

It might mean that he had the flexibility of movement around the town. More than likely, people would recognise him as Connie but not so much as Mark. And those that would know him as Mark were unlikely to be around in the daytime.

These were the people he would have to hunt down so he could begin to make amends with the past.

Unless of course it was already too late...

He would check social media later on in the safety of his hotel room and see if anything more had changed; unlikely it had, yet.

Social media – damn it, but bless it too.

People may not even remember him anymore. They had probably all moved on as well. True, somebody may one day think about those three drag queens that used to be on the stage at that cabaret bar, but would they ever really question what had happened to any of them?

Hmmm, probably not; most would probably still know where Tequila was though.

In fact, it hadn't taken much effort to find out what had become of Tequila. A quick social media search had revealed that she and Wendy were headlining a cabaret show in a new bar on East Green Street called The Queen's Legs.

With Wendy WolfWhistle? Seriously, how the heck had that even happened?

Previous internet searches undertaken had allowed him to follow the journey of Tequila's recovery following the Divas fire. It had been quite the news story at the time and regional and local news items were not difficult to find.

It was all available at just the touch of a few buttons for those who wanted to know, and he did want to know.

The hash tags about the police raid on the opening night had been a concern though.

That wasn't a publicity stunt, far from it. That was a warning and a very severe one at that.

And East Green Street, well, he knew exactly where that was. He had walked down it enough times; had even lived on it for a while; had performed business on it too or near it or thereabouts.

Mark felt he knew exactly where The Queens Legs cabaret bar was. He was convinced it was where that other pub had been with the pervy landlord.

What was it they called him again? Oh yes: Wayne the stain.

The Queen's Legs might have been his local in a different life, but not anymore. He was no longer from around these parts.

He no longer wanted to be a local in any sense of the word. Once he had concluded his business, he would leave and then he would never come back.

Yes, Mark was definitely not a local anymore.

But others may disagree, and they would disagree, for he was from around these parts and he was one of them.

And Mark may stop being a local through other means too, but for the moment it was his prerogative to turn his back on all of it.

The day after Bonfire night

Shaking his head in utter despair, Jay put away his mobile phone, sighed quite heavily, gritted his teeth and then carried on walking up the road alone.

All he wanted was to be left alone.

It wasn't too much to ask, was it?

He didn't need to keep being reminded of what was expected of him. He knew exactly what was expected of him.

Why did he need to be constantly reminded?

Why was he never allowed to forget anything? He would like to at least forget some of the things inside his head.

It wasn't going to be easy, it may even be ridiculously impossible but a plan was in place and that plan needed completing to the best of his ability.

And if that plan should falter in anyway, then he only had himself to blame. He was in charge of the plan; him and him alone. It was all in his hands and it was his destiny and sole desire to get exactly what he wanted.

It had been several hours since he had followed Oliver's Mother out of The Queen's Legs cabaret bar and up the street.

His head, now so full of new knowledge and change strategies, that he had needed some time out to digest it all and recompose himself.

It was most certainly tiring him out beyond belief.

So there were concerns in the wider world that Oliver was not responding to expected communications. He was not acting or behaving in a manner that was expected of him, and his Mother, out of everyone, should know that something was possibly amiss.

So the world was slowly waking up to the realisation that something was going on with Oliver. And not in a good way either.

But he would have to work around all that and he would have to make his plan work.

What else could he do? It was too late to change anything now.

Yes, he absolutely had to stick to the plan.

Nobody in the bar had seemed concerned by what had happened though. They had just acted as though this was the most normal thing in the world. As far as they were concerned he had quit his job the night before and had gone AWOL.

Hmmm, but a mysterious disappearance was far from normal.

He walked through a small passageway with random weeds growing through the cracks in the paving. It was between two blocks of flats, one of which looked as though it was long beyond help; where apparently Wayne from the pub lived.

He quickened his pace and found himself back on East Green Street.

He was as hungry as he was exhausted and he needed to get back to his new flat on East Green Street.

25k East Green Street to be precise.

The same block where Oliver lived, except Oliver didn't know that. He had no idea that they were sharing the same landlord, hallways, staircase and brightly painted, communal front door.

And why would Oliver need to know?

Oliver didn't particularly know any of his neighbours. Why would he need to know that the man who had been sitting and watching him whilst he worked at The Queen's Legs cabaret bar now lived in the same block as him?

Is that something he should have been aware of?

Jay put his key into his front door, turned the lock and entered his slightly chilly home. It wasn't particularly nice inside but it would do in the meantime.

Of course, it would probably help if he had unpacked even just a few of his personal belongings and put up a few pictures and such like; just to make it a little more homely; just to make living there that little bit more pleasant.

But he hadn't ever planned on living there for long.

Magnolia walls and brown carpets were pretty standard for rented accommodation the world over. It would certainly do in the meantime.

Once his tasks were concluded he would depart as silently as he had arrived; hopefully achieving what he had set out to do and better off for having done it, with exactly what he wanted.

But right now he would need to have just the shortest of sleeps to refresh his body, mind and soul for he hadn't slept much the night before and he didn't know when he might sleep next; possibly not the next night either.

There really was just way too much to think about with new and unanticipated information coming to his attention. His head hurt at the thought of it all.

Besides, it really was quite exhausting behaving in this way and he was really not used to being like this.

And he needed to stay on the top of his game, for people would get in his way and they would ask questions and he would have to try and deceive them all into thinking that nothing was amiss at all.

Thankfully his bed was the first thing he had put together when he had moved in. His bed was always ready for him, and as he yawned several times, he definitely felt it was calling him in.

But before the reality of sleep fully engulfed his very being; there was something he needed to do.

Something that if he didn't do would distract his slumber and now he needed to sleep. He needed to remove the mask that the outside world did not seem to know was there.

Out came coloured contact lenses which gave his eyes a completely different perspective, off came the cap and off came a short hairpiece that gave the affect of more hair than was actually there; for it was much shorter underneath.

He stared back in the mirror at himself; the real him - The man behind the disguise.

A wolf in sheep's clothing, perhaps?

He didn't even undress. He barely even found the energy to close the curtains, and as he lay there snuggled underneath the duvet, warm, comfortable and safe he found himself thinking about Oliver.

And as he drifted away, into a much-needed sleep, he still thought about the plan and Oliver.

Oh Oliver.

Oliver.

Oliver...

Back to late October

Chris stood on the edge of his glory.

The world was helping him achieve exactly what he requited and it was all coming together, just as he knew it would.

He welcomed the autumn sun beating down on his face with immense gratitude, whilst his pale skin trembled slightly for he had quickly grown too accustomed to the inside world and the shadows that cast darkness over everything.

It had really felt so claustrophobic; trapped inside those walls, festering, feeling as though nobody was listening to his cries for help.

A victim of his own misdemeanours.

The gentle breeze also tasted sweet against his lips and he inhaled too much too quickly, leaving him breathless but very much gasping for more.

But now the outside world with all its hopes and dreams and demons pulled him in.

How could he resist the temptations that lay in front of him?

How would he ever be able to turn his back on a free world? And it was a free world that lay in front of him, but for how long?

He wasn't used to being good, that was boring.

That was not for him.

He had never craved a life without colour.

He had never craved a life without excitement and power.

If they were his choices, then he might as well be back in his cell forever.

He might as well be dead.

BE CAREFUL WITH MY HEART

You played the game
And played to win
You ruled the world
Or so you thought you did

You brought the rainclouds
And chased the rainbows far away
You found my weak spots
Said you always would until my dying day

Just like a family torn apart
You can destroy my whole world too
I beg you...
Please, be careful with my heart

Don't leave me scared and alone this time
Don't leave me lost to find my own way home
Don't leave me cold

I saw your truth
I saw you fail
I knew you when
You tried to win but bailed

You made your sun set
And never wished upon that star
May God forgive you!
You're so far gone you don't know where you are

Just as the winds begin to change
And down falls the darkness once again
I beg you...
Please, be careful with my heart

And now I am scared and alone again
And I am too lost to find my own way home
And now I am cold

Trapped... inside your room of broken dreams
Believing... the net won't break your fall
Losing... all the hope you know you need to have
Waiting... for the one to set you free
Never knowing... that person could be me

Just when I thought the streets were safe
Now I'm afraid in case you're there
I beg you...
Please, be careful with my heart

You left me scared and alone once more
You left me lost to find my own way home
And now I am cold

And I beg you...
Please, be careful with my heart

And now I am cold
I'm cold
I'm cold

So very cold

"And now ladies and gentlemen please show your appreciation for your favourite night time TV host; the ex-hairdresser turned chat-show star who will always get to the root of the problem and blow your top, it's the one and only... Mrs Seavers!"

Mrs Seavers stepped out into the studio, which was part hair salon and part reception area to a large round of applause.

Her stunning brown hair was pulled majestically over one shoulder and trailed down her dress which dazzled like a million car lights driving across Spaghetti Junction in the night time.

She beamed widely at her audience and, as she always did, waved graciously to those in the back rows who hadn't arrived in enough time to get a better seat.

She sat herself down in the reception area and was handed a steaming cup of coffee by her 'Saturday girl' who then wandered into the background to fold freshly-laundered towels and rearrange the shampoos and conditioners before eventually disappearing out of sight altogether.

With her legs crossed and the tip of one of her raised high heels pointing upwards, she pouted somewhat seductively towards the camera, or at least she tried to, in an attempt to give the illusion that she was possibly a few years younger than she actually probably was.

And with her right hand she beckoned the camera to zoom out slightly from a dramatic close-up for she always felt that she looked better from a distance.

And that was another reason why she always waved graciously to those at the back because she knew she always looked her best to them.

She took a sip of her coffee and then placed it down on the coffee table in front of her. She ignored the selection of magazines laid out in a fan shape for her clients to peruse at their leisure.

After all, how many times can the same old story keep being told?

Boy meets girl.

Boy leaves girl.

Girl has really bad hair and urgently needs a makeover and contact lenses.

"And welcome to the Mrs Seavers show," she finally said. "I'm Mrs Seavers and this is my show.

"Well, tonight we have quite a different show for you by our usual standards. Joining me in the salon later will be the Psychic Drag Queen Miss April Showers and she is going to be predicting this summer's hottest new hairdos including, believe it or not, a new blonde and auburn streaked bouffant for a very elderly member of the royal family.

"I think you'll agree we would all love to see that on our bank notes.

"But first on the show we are going to tackle the very difficult subject of ladies who love then live to regret it. Sad tales of lonely, desperate women, who reach out to foreign, younger men, invest their life savings and then never see them again.

"So let's have a large round of applause for my first client in the salon tonight who is here to tell us all about how her Turkish delight gave her the chop."

At first, the audience clapped politely as they anticipated hearing about another sad old cow who would sit there sipping her coffee and munching on free custard creams whilst shedding a few tears for her lost lover and streaking through her very heavily over-applied makeup that was supposed to stop them looking so washed-out.

Hmmm, the same old story being told again, no doubt?

Another sad old cow who would relentlessly try to convince them that her nineteen year old Turkish lover was different from all the others, and as they genuinely loved each other, she felt she could legitimately give him the twenty five thousand pounds that he so urgently needed to save his Grandmother's leg from gangrene.

The same old story... yet again.

But the same old story isn't what came bouncing into the studio.

And the same old story isn't what came crashing down with great force on the sofa right next to Mrs Seavers making everything bounce upwards with the impact, including the host's very own personal particulars.

"Now, Mrs S, less of the desperate and lonely if you don't mind. As you can probably tell, I am far from that."

And her guest was instantly distracted by the fan of magazines on the coffee table in front of her.

"Ooh, I haven't read this one yet," she announced picking one up and quickly shoving it into her handbag. "You don't mind if I take it, do you? Saves me buying it and after my dreadful ordeal with my Turkish lover, I feel as though I barely have two pennies to rub together.

"Now where is my Coffee? I was promised coffee, you know, biscuits too. It's one of the reasons I'm here and to meet you, of course."

Mrs Seavers smiled politely at the over-sized troll in front of her; even though that probably wasn't the reaction she would have given had the cameras not been on her.

She explained that her 'Saturday girl' would be along presently with a hot beverage and a selection of biscuits, as promised.

"Now tell me all about your hideous ordeal, my dear. Obviously the entire experience has been... well, absolutely ghastly for you. To be honest, I don't know how you must have coped.

"Now, I suppose what my studio audience want to know as well as my viewers at home, is how you could even find the strength to come here today."

"Well, I suppose my hideous ordeal started this morning when I woke up and it just looked like this. Honestly, I can't do a thing with it," she replied. "If I lose one more hairbrush in it I'm going to start looking like a hairdresser's Christmas tree that should probably belong in Dracula's palace.

"Oh, but I do like your hair though, Mrs S. You have lovely hair. Could I borrow it after the show?"

"Erm no, this is my hair. Now let's get back onto the subject of... okay, let's call it your other ordeal then. Now you initially met Ibrahim online, didn't you?"

"That's right, and I still can't believe he deceived me."

"Well, some might say that you were not entirely honest with the truth yourself. Now was it or was it not a picture of Kylie Minogue from circa 2004 that you used as your profile picture to entice, and I'm using your words here, a swarm of international bees to your honey making pollen?"

"Oh but everybody lies a little bit online and just slightly exaggerates their own photo. I mean it's expected when you date online. Even my friend Miss Sugar Daddy does it because she airbrushes her moustache off and believe me that hairy beast is not going anywhere in real life. The poor thing, she hasn't been blessed with the lady bum fluff that you can simply foundation away; like we have."

"Now Wendy, isn't it true that you didn't tell anybody about what happened between

170

yourself and Ibrahim because you were so mortified by what happened that you simply couldn't face the embarrassment and humiliation of it all?"

"Erm, no not quite. I actually didn't tell anybody because I was too busy preparing for the Divas Beauty (drag) Queen contest. I won, you know. In fact, I'm going to headline the cabaret show this very weekend. Will you be able to pop along to Divas Cabaret bar and watch me? I can ask Chris to put your name on the guest list, but it may already be full though."

"Possibly not, but thank you anyway."

The 'Saturday girl' put down a steaming cup of coffee in front of her, which she immediately picked up and took a large swig from. It was, after all, thirsty work being on a popular, late night chat show that barely anybody watched.

"Oh Mrs S, I do like your shoes; they're utterly charming. Do you know, I was going to buy the exact same pair too but they simply were not designed for a slimmer width and everywhere I put my foot the blasted things flew right off, can you believe it?

"Do you like my new shoes? I bought them off the internet. They used to belong to Cinderella."

(Or at least one of her ugly step-sisters.)

Mrs Seavers turned to the camera and grinned. "Other made up fairytales are also available. Okay, now let's get back to your relationship with Ibrahim."

"Or as I very much like to call him now: Ihatehim!"

"So when did you suspect that he was only in a relationship with you for your money?"

"I think it was when he arrived for the very first time at my front door and demanded twenty pounds for the taxi fare."

"And from that moment you never had a moment's peace, did you? And I understand Ibrahim wasn't just demanding money from you, was he?"

"No, he wasn't, Mrs S. He wanted a takeaway too."

"And I understand that this must be so very, very difficult for you, but is it true that he even withheld sex unless you gave him more money?"

"Well, yes and no to that question. Although if I am being completely honest probably not so much withholding sex but more so telling me that no amount of money in the world would make him want to sleep with me."

"And that must have come as quite a shock to you?"

"You can say that again because I went on to win the Divas Beauty (drag) Queen contest. Did I already mention that?"

"In passing perhaps, but whilst we're on that subject is it true that Ibrahim took so much of your money that you could barely afford anything decent to wear for this drag queen beauty pageant and you turned up looking like something you would put out in the meadow to scare away the birds?"

"No, I don't recall that being the case at all," she squealed whilst fingering through the selection of biscuits in front of her. "Now somebody backstage said that sometimes you have shortbread and I don't mean to sound rude, but I'm still waiting for some. I like a nice bit of shortbread.

"But I'll pop some of these other biscuits in my bag for later. Do you like my bag? It used to belong to Whitney Houston."

"Okay, we'll see what we can do about that, but what we all really want to know, what we all really need to know is how much money did Ibrahim take from you in the end?"

"Just the twenty pounds for the taxi fare. I thought I'd already mentioned that. But what you will want to know and this is where it gets very exciting..."

"Oh yes."

"He didn't even bring me flowers. Now who goes on a first date empty handed. I mean I know I'm not quite Kylie Minogue, but he didn't know that."

"So are you telling me that your Turkish lover Ibrahim went back to Turkey after just one date with only twenty pounds of your money?"

"No, not back to Turkey, just to West Green Street. It's literally only about five minutes from my gorgeous, little studio flat. Honestly, it would never have cost that much in a taxi from his to mine and he could just as easily have walked it, if the truth be told."

"I think we've heard enough now. Let's go to a commercial break."

And Wendy WolfWhistle stood up and took a bow. She may not have been what the producers or Mrs Seavers were expecting but to the audience she had been a big success and they had been thoroughly entertained by her.

"Is it okay if I stick around?" she asked between filming, "I'd love to meet the Psychic Drag Queen. What did you say her name was again: Miss April Showers? Oh how very unimaginative. Did she come up with that in the bathroom or in the month of?"

"I really don't know," replied Mrs Seavers, still slightly disarrayed by the torpedo that had whirly twirled through her studio.

Torpedo Wendy, no less.

"Now, Mrs Seavers is there any chance you might want to give me the slightest of demi-wave perms after I've met April. There's a drinks promotion down at Divas cabaret bar tonight and I want to look my best as it might be busy. April might want to come with me."

It was quite unlikely any of that was ever going to happen.

It was even more unlikely that Wendy would go on to make the grade for the episode that would be aired later that week, but it had been great fun and she wouldn't know she had been cut until after she had invited a select few around to her dimly lit studio flat for an intimate viewing including Chris Randall, Jake Robinson and Miss Tittie Mansag; fortunately, none of whom would show up anyway.

Hmmm, now maybe she could sell her story to the nationals. They would probably pay more too; more than a cup of coffee, a few biscuits (not shortbread) and a copy of some magazine that would contain a riveting article about cervical cancer which she would then go on to think she may have, momentarily.

But first she would hang around the back corridors and look up this Psychic Drag Queen Miss April Showers. She felt sure they would become fast friends. Providing that was, that this Miss April Showers didn't look better than she did in drag.

Which again was very unlikely.

Otherwise, she might just have to heavy rain all over her showery parade and ruin her life.

And that was probably more likely.

Q💔 CHAPTER 27 Q💔

Bonfire night

...Oliver heard the noise again; louder this time.

Oh, it's the bloody fireworks outside. Thank God for that.

Okay, so you're a lager barrel and you're probably something else. So then what are you?

Hmmm, can I seriously be arsed with this? At worst if I manage to make this work, cider will probably flow through the lager pump. At best, Wayne will have to change the lager himself.

That really would be the easiest option.

Actually resigning would be the easiest option.

He knew what he had to do...

What with the noise of the fireworks on the street outside and with a mixture of Oliver's fear for being down there and trying to make a bad situation better or worse, he hadn't noticed that the cellar door had slowly opened and somebody had slipped inside and had snuck quietly down the stone steps and had joined him in the bleak, cold underworld.

He didn't hear whoever this person was approach him from behind because they had walked slowly and carefully across the concrete floor.

And, just as the loudest and longest firework seemed to scream through the night sky outside, he didn't hear the movement of the weapon that was used to strike him hard from behind.

He fell onto the hard barrels and landed awkwardly in a very uncomfortable position, but that didn't matter for he was knocked out unconscious.

And nobody had heard him scream in pain, bar for the person who was in the cellar with him.

And nobody had seen him fall, bar for the person who was in the cellar with him.

And nobody had seen him being pulled out of view and dragged to his Hell, bar for the person who was in the cellar with him.

And nobody knew where he had gone or where he was, bar for the person who was in the cellar with him.

Early November.

Just before the evening's cabaret show was about to begin, Tequila knocked on the door of Martin's office.

James always felt more confident with his mask on and had decided to broach a number of issues that were on his mind dressed as her.

In a way, he hoped that Martin would find Tequila more formidable and perhaps be more accommodating of the situations.

Money! Fame! Truth!

"Come in," replied Martin's voice from behind the closed door.

Tequila opened the door and stepped inside. It was the first time back in there since that night when the secrets within the drawers had been revealed.

In fact, it was the first time even just standing at the door for any period of time since hearing Wendy and Martin talking, perhaps not as quietly as they might have thought they were, about Jake, the night of the Divas fire and what may or may not have happened or been seen.

"Ahhh Tequila," said Martin as she entered the room, "what can I do for you?"

As he always seemed to do when somebody was in there with him, he pushed gently on his desk drawers to ensure they were as fully closed as they could be.

He was always very discrete about it and nobody ever noticed what he was doing.

But of course, Tequila's mindset went straight to the desk drawers and she may even have noticed Martin's slight arm movement as he undertook the routine of checking that they were fully closed yet again.

"Can we talk?" she asked him.

"Yes of course," he replied and gestured her towards a seat opposite him. "What's on your mind?"

"The night of the Divas fire..." she began to say.

"What about it?"

"I thought I saw Jake Robinson standing in the distance."

"No, you couldn't have done. Jake was dead by then."

Tequila sat and stared at the overweight, bald man sitting across the desk from her. So, he was playing the same cards for her that he had played with Wendy.

Hmmm, maybe it was time to shuffle the deck?

"No, I definitely saw Jake," she said more firmly.

"No, you couldn't have done," repeated Martin even more firmly than that.

How had this conversation come to light twice now in less than a few days. Had Wendy and her son been speaking about it together?

"You were obviously traumatised by the effects of the smoke," he continued to say. "That's probably what it was; hallucinations and all."

"Yes, maybe," said Tequila, although she remained far from convinced about it.

Why was Martin adamant that Jake could not have been there that night? True, he had died before the night of the fire and Chris Randall had been arrested for his murder. I mean Chris had even admitted it in the Divas dressing room; they had all heard him, but something just wasn't adding up somewhere.

"Was there anything else?" Martin asked, hoping that there wouldn't be.

Money! Fame! Truth!

"I'm sorry, but I truly believe that I saw Jake that night, and I don't understand why you keep dismissing it. It's pretty uncool of you to dismiss the possibility, if you ask me."

Martin stopped looking at her and turned his face towards his computer screen and began tapping away on the keyboard. He may have been pretending. "Shouldn't you be helping wedge Wendy into a corset right about now?" he asked.

Money! Fame! Truth!

"Probably," replied Tequila. "And just so you know, I did see Jake that night and I know that Wendy did too. You can't keep fobbing us

180

both off. I don't believe he is dead, not for a moment."

"I want you to go now," said Martin. "And I think you should watch your step very carefully."

"I wear high heels for six hours a day," replied Tequila flippantly, "I always have to watch my step."

"I'm warning you, Tequila. I hired you and I can just as easily fire you. Is that what you want?"

No, that isn't what Tequila wanted at all; far from it.

Money! Fame! Truth!

"Right, then let's not say anything more about this," said Martin calmly. "Jake is dead and there is nothing any of us can do about it, no matter how much we wish differently. It's very sad but unfortunately it's true."

"I know," said Tequila backing down slightly. "I didn't really know Jake that well, but he seemed like a really nice bloke. Perhaps I am just wishful thinking."

And again, Tequila was not entirely convinced by the conversation they were having.

Money! Fame! Truth!

And then she played her trump card...

"Of course, if I did know some secrets, Martin, I wonder how much my silence would be worth."

"What secrets do you know?" asked Martin, instantly going into police mode.

"I know about your little secret for a start," she replied. "The one you keep tightly locked away inside your desk drawer."

Money! Fame! Truth!

But she played her trump card too early...

"I don't know how you know or what you think you know, but I won't be blackmailed, not anymore, and especially not by somebody like you."

He paused for breath; his whole body raging with adrenaline and anger.

Had this scrawny, lanky piece of crap seriously just tried to blackmail him?

"If I was you, Tequila," he continued to say, "I would shut up now before it's too late. Seriously, I'm warning you, if this matter is ever raised again you will be out of here before your high heels can touch the ground. Do you understand me?"

Tequila sat there slightly trembling. This clearly hadn't gone the way she had perceived at all.

Had she been too naive to think that Martin would gasp in horror and pay her thousands of pounds to keep quiet about the secret arrangement that lay hidden in his desk drawer?

In hindsight, she probably hadn't thought this through enough.

"Now go," said Martin, "and if I hear any of this stupidity again then I mean it, you're out on your arse; homeless, broke and unemployed."

Tequila stood up and left the room without making any eye contact with him.

He was right; she had been utterly stupid about this. She was too young to play a grown up man's game.

She thought she could play to win, but she lost and she had almost lost everything.

Stupidity...

Yes, she was stupid and she knew it.

But Martin had been even more stupid.

He had made secret arrangements with Chris Randall.

Seriously, what had he been thinking?

Chris Randall of all people.

And now... a short intermission

"Hi there, I'm Miss Shimmy Shoo and you probably best know me from starring in 'The Black Queen'.

"Today I am going to tell you all about my fabulicious new album.

"What's that I hear you cry, there is no way I can better my previous eponymously-titled top 100 charting album, oh but dear fans I have.

"My new album titled *I've got the shimmy shimmy shakes,* includes all your favourite Shimmy-related tracks, for example: Blue Suede Shoos, Crocodile Shoos and my personal favourite Miss Goody two Shoos, hey that's me.

"Oh for goodness sakes, *I've got the shimmy shimmy shakes* is available in participating retailers now, whilst stocks last.

"So what are you waiting for? Let's face the shoo-sic and dance."

And back to July

His visitor stared once more around the cold, walls of the room and shuddered to himself slightly.

It was a feeling like somebody had just walked over his grave. Oddly, an expression he had never really understood before, but now he seemed to get it.

He really seemed to get it.

He shuddered once more. This time it was more apparent to the person sitting in front of him. He really didn't like this. He didn't like any part of this at all nor, he very much suspected, would he like what was about to come.

He knew Chris was not going to back down, especially when he had so much to gain.

He knew that Chris would peck away at him until every morsel had been consumed and every bone was clean and he was sitting pretty once again; grooming his feathers at the very top of the food chain.

And there was very little he could do to prevent any of this happening.

"To be honest with you," replied Chris, "I couldn't care less what you think. You screwed me over and this is what we are going to do about it."

His visitor listened carefully to every single word spoken and did not enjoy hearing any part of it.

"No," he bravely responded once Chris had finished what was clearly a very well-prepared and overly rehearsed speech.

So this is what he had been doing every night in his prison cell; practising for this moment.

Chris stared coolly back at him and once more ensured he captured his gaze. This was the response he had expected, but it was not the outcome he knew he would finally receive in the end.

Chris always got what he wanted and he knew this would be no exception to the precedence already set so many times beforehand.

"No," responded his visitor again.

Chris stared back at him. Although not speaking a single word, his silence said everything that required hearing. He folded his arms again, tighter than he had done before and continued to stare. He once again reiterated all of his demands.

"For the final time, Martin," he said, "this is what is going to happen.

"You will open your silly little pub on the corner of East Green Street and you will call it whatever you want, it doesn't matter because it'll get changed again in due course. Call it The Queen's Legs for all I care. Hmmm, actually, I can just see the puns now; the grand opening of The Queen's Legs; people will come just to say that.

"You will hire that Tequila thing as the lead cabaret star, oh and book in Wendy too; they'll

186

be good enough to keep the audiences piling in, in the short term anyway, especially Wendy. She'll be so bad that she'll be good. Let Wendy think she's the lead, she'll love that.

"You will be the face of the pub. Do you think you can manage that? Not an ideal choice I know but beggars can't be choosers, right?

"So, as I explained before, right about when you seemed to stop listening to me, the pub will not be yours; it will be mine. Your name can go above the door initially, but once I am out of here it will be all mine. A little nest egg, let's call it.

"Everybody can think that it's yours, nobody needs to know the truth, well, not yet anyway. And then when I do get out of here I will take over once more.

"Oh, and then you lot will all be out on your arses, but you had probably gathered that.

"Ideally, you need somebody behind the scenes who knows what they're doing. Find out what the old landlord is doing these days. From what I know about the dirty old pervert; he'll fit right in there."

This was now the second time that Martin had heard all of this and it was still very difficult to digest; Chris was after the pub that he was in the process of opening.

No, he wasn't just after it, he was demanding it. And Martin knew that he would take it if he wanted it. Martin had screwed up big time and Chris knew it.

Chris really did have all the winning cards no matter what game they played.

This time, Martin was more engaged; there was no point angering the situation anymore than it already was. "So the money for the investment..." he began to say.

"Will be mine," quickly interrupted Chris, "Eventually." Then he smiled; a sneaky smile that instantly sent further shivers through Martin's soul.

"Eventually?" questioned Martin. "What is that supposed to mean?"

Chris continued to stare right back at him and smiled once more sending a ricochet of chills through Martin's anxious body and desperate mind.

"Well, as you can imagine, being stuck in here isn't exactly lucrative, although you wouldn't believe some of the things that the men get up to in here just for a bit of cash, you know just to make their experience in here that little bit more bearable. Sometimes just for a bit of sex in the shower block.

"You know, it's a pity you're not in here, Martin. You could get a bit too and sometimes for just as little as a packet of cigarettes, sometimes even half a packet if they're really desperate, and let's face it, they would have to be."

"Just get to the point, will you?" snapped Martin.

He didn't care for this mindless chit chat; he just needed to know the facts that affected him and his new business venture.

It was obvious though that Chris was playing him like a violin, plucking him, pulling at his strings, working him harder and harder until something broke.

Guaranteed, sweet, sweet music was not being made.

"Have you heard of Spice?" Chris continued to say, "It's like a synthetic version of cannabis; they're going mad for it in here. It even turns some of them mad. I don't get involved myself, I've got too much sense for that, but some of them pay through the nose for it.

"Incidentally, that's how some of them get their stuff in here; through the nose. It's a very under-estimated orifice. Did you know that?"

"Yes I know that," replied Martin. I was in the police force."

"But you're not in the police force anymore though, are you, Martin? Did you resign before you were pushed out?"

"You don't know anything about that situation."

"You'll be surprised what I do know. From what I've heard, you shouldn't have been undercover in Divas. You shouldn't have arrested me. You were told to stay out of it as you were too closely involved in the situation. They really have had to cover up your mishaps big time, haven't they?"

Martin didn't say anything. He had messed up and on a mammoth scale too and the police were still covering it all up now, or rather trying to sort it all out.

"From what I have gathered, you took the role of a bent copper just that little bit too far, didn't you?"

"Who is telling you all of this? I demand you tell me."

"You don't get to make the demands, Martin. Not now. Not anymore. I'm the boss of you now. You do everything that I tell you to do.

"Now, did you do it because you got beaten up outside Divas or did you do it because you secretly loved wearing your mother's old tat? I reckon it was the latter one."

"Right, I've had enough of this," exclaimed Martin, just loud enough for the prison officers to look over, but not enough to make them intervene. "Just tell me how this all affects me and cut out the bollocks, okay?"

Chris was still smiling. He was enjoying this so much more than he thought he would be. Ha, this was such great payback for that vile, rancid old queen who had been undercover in his cabaret bar watching his every move. Well, he would regret that now.

"Do you miss the police force, Martin?"

Martin looked around the room. He didn't miss dealing with the perpetrators for a second. He didn't miss the verbal abuse and the horrific stories, but generally he did miss the job a lot.

It was his life and it had been taken away from him all because of Chris Randall. And now, as he was rising once more from his ashes, Chris Randall was about to take his new venture away from him too.

Seriously, how was this man not dead?

Seriously, how had somebody not come along already and shot him down?

For God's sake he was in prison! He was supposed to be restricted; he was supposed to be banned from the outside world, but here he was still pulling all the strings like the ultimate puppet master.

Somebody on the outside must be helping him?

But who?

Martin found just an ounce of inner strength. But if he wanted to get out of there and away from him and this situation then he needed to find a lot more and quickly.

"It's going to be so great on the outside," said Chris thoughtfully. "A new business, a new start and maybe even a new love. How is Oliver these days?"

"Leave Oliver out of this. He's suffered enough because of you."

"He's barely suffered at all," snapped back Chris, "Oh, and give that little shit a job too; just the weekends will be fine. I want him behind that bar so I know exactly where he is when I need to look him up.

"I'm sure the punters will spend their money frivolously just to get a closer look at him, maybe even a wink or a slight touch. That's what I used to say about Jake too and it worked, for most of the time."

Martin exhaled deeply and re-broached the previous subject again. "What about the investment for the business?" That was all he cared about now.

"Oh yes," said Chris, rubbing his hands together gleefully, "I'm glad we're back onto that. So, I know all about the inheritance that your Mother left you in her will. Bingo wins, a reasonable house to sell..."

"You're not having it," announced Martin bravely interrupting him. "It's mine, for my future. You're not having any of it."

"I could have your soul if I wanted it, Martin."

Martin looked down in dismay. Chris was right, he probably could. "And the investment?" he whispered.

"Your money initially and then you sign it all over to me. Oh, don't worry; you won't be out of pocket. It won't be long before I get the insurance money from Divas; my legal team are on it right now. Have you come across them yet? No, I don't suppose you have, but you will. They're truly amazing. And do expect a call from them in the near future; they think I have a great case to get out of here, but you would already know that, wouldn't you?

"Oh, and I'm selling my house too; that'll be another little nest egg for me, so I will need to move into the accommodations above my new cabaret bar when the time comes."

Martin ignored him. He didn't care about Chris's house but he did care about his own assets. "So when you get your insurance money sorted out, I get my investment back?"

It didn't seem ideal, but it could be a way out of it all. Perhaps he could cut his losses and run away once and for all. Get out of this town and to someplace new where nobody knew him, nobody could blackmail him and nobody could take away everything that was rightfully his.

"Oh no," replied Chris, "quite the opposite really."

"What? I don't understand."

"My insurance payout will be tied back up in that Divas building. It will only be available in that wretched building that almost destroyed me. That is what you will get."

"So I will get the old Divas building and you will get The Queen's Legs, as you have suggested it might be called?"

Chris nodded. "And you'll get a bit of a building makeover too; I won't leave you completely high and dry. I know it's in the arse end of town but, you know, it's better than the truth coming out, isn't it? You can always sell the lease on. It would make a great casino or nightclub or something. To be honest, I don't really care what you do with it. I just want shut of the place."

"And let's suppose I agree to this..."

"Which you will," interrupted Chris.

"What will I get in return?"

"This will all go away for you. I may even go away for you too."

His visitor sat silently for a few moments, trying his hardest to stare at him in the eyes.

If he could do that then he could do this.

Finally he nodded. It was a no-win situation whichever way he cut the cake, but the thought of Chris never crossing his path again seemed a possibility that he felt had to be the journey he needed to take.

"And just one more thing," said Chris, smiling widely.

Martin looked at him.

For fucks sake, what now?

"I've suddenly grown rather fond of the name The Queen's Legs. Please call it that. At least until I get there."

Martin stood up and left, without any further acknowledgment.

The Queen's Legs was his for now, but how long would it be his for?

More importantly, Chris had indicated that these prison walls may not be able to hold him for much longer.

But when the Hell would that day come?

Q❤ CHAPTER 30 Q❤

The day after Bonfire night

Mark (AKA Connie) anxiously entered the Northern Territory of town. In actual fact, he was terrified. It had been a while since he'd had both the confidence and the die-hard attitude to grace these dismal streets.

It was the worst place to be and not somewhere you ever went to unless you needed rent boys, a dose of campylobacter or something very unpleasant to happen to Chris Randall.

It was also notorious for drug abuse too, but you only ever used in the Northern Territory, you never sold. For there was only one seller and everybody who needed to know knew exactly whose job that was...

The Maniac!

You never crossed The Maniac, let alone double cross him.

It was not a nice place to be and Mark felt chilled through just from being back there, as the memories of his past haunted him once more. This had once been the centre of his darkness and he was determined to ensure that this was absolutely the last visit he ever made there.

But he had already vowed all of this and here he was breaking those vows already.

Once he was out of there, he would wipe the slate clean, cross the line and never look back. In his mind, he would always know it was there but he may not always know how to find it.

Hopefully, in time it would be shut down and it would move on and then he would never really know again, but for now he knew exactly what was what.

He just hoped that he could still negotiate a deal.

If you ever need to find the Northern Territory then head towards where Divas cabaret bar used to be, take the second left at the end of the road by the crumbling old church and keep going until you can hear the screams; until you can taste the smell of burnt out cars and you can feel the fear.

He spotted his destination. It wasn't difficult to find as it had remained unchanged for quite some time now. Even the untrained amateur walking by on the pavement and who just happened to glance through the window of 76 North Town Street could see that there was something different about it; for it certainly stood out from the rest of the terraced row.

For a start, it was clean and tidy and immaculately presented. The blinds at the window hung with perfect horizontal latitude and two shiny, ceramic flower pots housed winter blooms with trailing Ivy on either side of the doorway.

Mark's instinct was almost to stop and smell the flowers. They looked like Viola or Winter Pansies, he wasn't sure. But he hadn't come to the best dressed secret in town to admire their colourful and pretty, little faces.

He had come to meet The Maniac, and his face was far from pretty.

Mark pushed the door open and stepped inside. The familiar smells and sights surrounded his senses once more and for a moment it felt as though he had never been away.

The place always smelt of fresh flowers and coffee, as though the sweetness and the flavours were there to entice you in further.

It was the strangest of insides, it wasn't a house in the sense of it being a home, nor was it a business. It was merely a destination which many reached and most couldn't wait to leave.

The Maniac was greatly feared and even at this stage in the process, Mark considered walking away but he was already there and his conscience would soon drag him back.

It was now or later.

There was no now or never.

And he was back in his Hell.

It was primarily a two up, two down with a kitchen in the second downstairs room and an office upstairs. The front room, were Mark now stood, was nothing but painted cream, wooden floor boards and cream woodchip wallpaper.

A desk sat in the corner with a vase of fresh flowers on it and a Cheese Plant to its side which was long overdue re-staking.

Mark had never seen anybody sitting at the desk, although he had seen one of the Heavies reluctantly watering the plant and changing the flowers.

Between the two downstairs rooms was a steep flight of stairs which led the way to a tiny landing, just big enough for two doors to lead off in either direction.

One door led to the room were the Heavies hung out and also doubled up as a waiting room for any visitor that The Maniac felt required intimidation. The cream painted woodchip walls followed upwards too.

The other door led directly to The Maniac, and usually to several other Heavies who were protecting him, drinking with him or receiving their instructions, for example to burn down Divas night club.

In theory, it was a tiny space for such monstrous beings and the downstairs space was mostly unused. It didn't make sense, none of it, but this was the world according to The Maniac and not Mark's to amend or enhance in anyway.

He pushed open the door and there inside, as he expected there to be, sat The Maniac behind a very grand desk. Two Heavies stood either side of him and bar for a large, metal safe and a silver picture frame facing away from him, the room looked exactly like the one downstairs.

"Well, well, well," he exclaimed upon seeing Mark entering the room for the first time in months. "I was wondering if I was ever going to see you again."

He turned to his Heavies and ushered them out of the room, so they were both alone.

"I see you haven't brought the twins with you this time," he continued to say, beckoning towards Mark's flat chest area with his eyes and forehead. "Such a shame, I used to find them quite fascinating. Left them at home, have you?"

"Yes, something like that," Mark replied, trying to appear calmer and more in control than he was actually feeling.

"So what do you want?" asked The Maniac.

The pleasantries had been made. They had caught up with each other's news, of sorts. Now it was time to get down to business.

It had been a while since Mark had needed to go into this zone and he was not used to it, especially as Mark, for Mark was never as confident or as edgy as Connie ever was. And now he missed that mask.

He missed the thick layer of makeup that nobody could ever see through.

He missed the shadows and the darkness that he could hide away within.

He suddenly wished he was a hundred miles away.

And that is what The Maniac and the Northern Territory did to even the most determined of people.

It broke them.

Q💔 CHAPTER 31 Q💔

Back to early November

Tequila was not on her best form.

In fact, Tequila was remarkably quiet and slightly downcast for once. Even a bad day for Tequila was usually more upbeat than a good day for most.

Wendy had shown her the fan letter she had received. Well, less so shown, more so shoved it into her face as she was in the process of sweeping off the excess after baking her makeup for the required ten or so minutes for that much sought after creaseless effect.

And unlike Wendy, and more like Martin, she knew this was not good.

♫ *Oh, uh-uh-uh, oh*

You are my playboy
Stay boy
Every night and day boy

Treat me bad
Treat me good
Treat me like you know you should

You have the power in your hands
You're the emperor of my lands
Touch me there
If you dare
You can have me anywhere

Oh, uh-uh-uh, oh ♫

It was just a little bit too surreal because Tequila had also received a letter too, and just

200

as Wendy's had arrived, by hand and through the letter box.

But unlike Wendy, she had not shown it to anybody and nobody but her and whoever had sent it even knew it existed.

Of course, that was before she knew what was in Wendy's letter. Now, in hindsight, hers seemed much worse than she had initially contemplated.

♫ *But don't tell me that you love me*
That isn't what I'm looking for

I just want some...
Pure adulteration
In my room
No complication
Take me as you find me
Take me as I am ♫

'Enjoy your performance; you never know when it might be your last.'

Short and to the point.

♫ *Oh, uh-uh-uh, oh*

Have you no shame, boy?
Game boy
Aren't you pleased you came, boy?

Don't stop now
See it through
If you know what's good for you

I know exactly what to do
To make all your dreams come true
You can stay
Everyday
When you rub me the right way

Oh, uh-uh-uh, oh ♫

What did it all mean? Was her past catching up with her? Was Wendy being threatened too because they were Father and Son? Did they come as a package these days?

Why were they both being targeted? Who had anything to gain from them both being out of the picture?

♫ *But don't tell me that you love me*
That isn't what I'm looking for

I just want some...
Pure adulteration
In my room
No complication
Take me as you find me
Take me as I am

I just want your...
Endless need to please me
All the time
'til you release me
Take me cos you want me
Take me as I am ♫

Don't take me as I am.

Certainly not because you want to kill me, that's for sure.

Enjoy your performance; you never know when it might be your last...

What did it all mean?

Q💔 CHAPTER 32 Q💔

The day after Bonfire night

Oliver opened his eyes and muttered something quite incomprehensible as he came to.

But nobody heard him.

He had no idea where he was or indeed what had happened to him or even how long he had been there for.

His head was hurting and he couldn't remember why.

It could have been any time of the day or night; for the room was cold and in absolute darkness. He tried to adjust his vision to accommodate the blackness that surrounded him but it was no good, he could not see a thing.

All he knew is that he was lying on a hard floor which felt rough and uneven, it might have been concrete but it could just as easily have been something else that had perhaps weathered over the years.

He could also feel something tight and restrictive over his mouth which pulled on his cheeks and skin as he tried to open his mouth to shout out for help.

Of course, instinctively he tried to remove whatever was there but he couldn't for he had been tied tightly around the wrists and his fingers were firstly numb and then they tingled with pins and needles. His ankles were tied tightly together too.

He was completely captured and there was nothing he could do to help himself.

He didn't even know how large or small the place he was in was.

He was starving, thirsty and he had possibly soiled himself too for his crotch area felt wet and cold.

What had happened?

He remembered that he had been in the cellar changing the lager barrel. Okay, not so much changing it but more so fannying around and trying to make quick life decisions whilst fireworks were going off outside.

Yes, it was bonfire night.

Was it still bonfire night?

He tried to listen hard but he couldn't hear anything; certainly not fireworks; certainly not anything.

There was only silence and darkness.

Where the Hell was he?

He tried to adjust his vision to see if he could make out anything; even just a single something that would give him a clue as to his whereabouts, but he couldn't see anything in any direction.

There was possibly a door somewhere.

If there was a door could he escape through it? But what was beyond the door was possibly only darkness too.

He presumed he was still underground as the air felt musty and cold.

Yes, he must still be in the cellars.

Who would have done this to him? The only person who may have had any desire to see him suffer like this was Chris Randall and it was unlikely to be him, right?

For he was safely locked away, wasn't he?

Doesn't this type of thing only ever happen in the movies or in over dramatised soap operas? It certainly didn't happen to the likes of him and certainly not in his world anyway.

As he lay there silently, a very slight sliver of light appeared very low to the ground; possibly at the bottom of a door.

Hopefully it meant somebody was nearby.

But maybe it was whoever had done this to him; the person who had attacked him in the first place and had left him to his own torment.

That person would certainly know where he was and that somebody was even there.

"Help," he screamed as loudly as he could, but it came out mostly muffled and extremely distorted.

He tried to scream louder and louder but nothing that made any sense, other than what was inside his own head spilled out.

He needed whoever was there to hear him, if indeed there was somebody there. He needed them to know where he was. He needed them to help him.

And if the person standing out there was the one who had done this to him, then so be it.

After all, he had nothing more to lose.

Nobody responded to his desperate plea for help, but the door began to open and the room he was in quickly lit up by the light from the adjourning room.

Oliver blinked, for the shift from darkness to light had temporarily distracted his vision.

There was definitely somebody standing there, staring back at him as he lay helplessly in this, what he could now see, was a small room made of bricks and cracked cement and mortis and most definitely still within the cellars.

He saw their silhouette first and then as he grew accustomed to the light, he began to see who it was.

Standing there at the door looking down at him was Jay.

Q❤ CHAPTER 33 Q❤

And back to July

He really didn't like this at all.

He felt very ill at ease inside this type of environment, breathless even as the walls seemed to close in on him and the darkness began to engulf him. But he needed to do this if he was ever to get what he wanted.

And he really wanted to get what he wanted.

The smells, the sounds, the other faces all staring back at him; how could anybody endure this situation. What would lead anybody to put themselves at risk and end up like this?

Maybe, like him, they just really wanted to get what they wanted.

But unlike all of them, he would get what he wanted and live to reap the rewards; he would not suffer the consequences.

And unlike all of them, he would get away with it too.

And Chris Randall was going to help him do it.

***

Chris was already sitting in the visitor's room waiting for him to arrive; hopefully this one would be instantly more forthcoming than the one who had visited him the day beforehand.

But either way, they were both going to do exactly as he said.

Chris looked around the room; it really was quite an unimpressive sight. The day before he had barely even had time to notice anything; his ultimate goal had been to wear him down and he had; this time he noticed the grim furnishing, the faded red chairs, the notice boards and a cobweb up high.

He grimaced after a very large man nearby winked hopefully at him.

The last time they had met, Chris had needed to undertake quite an unsavoury task on him; something he never would have done in the real world, but he needed a mobile phone and there was no other way of getting his hands on one given his current status.

Guaranteed there would not be a repeat performance of that with him or anybody else in there, regardless of how good he was told he had been.

He only needed that mobile for one call and one call only and then it would be disposed of, forever out of sight, forever out of mind; hopefully just like the memories of that god-awful experience.

Chris shuddered, and looked away. Just like his last visitor had been with him; he could not make eye contact. He didn't want to. He didn't need to. They had both got out of the arrangement what they wanted; the deal was done. The cards were firmly back in the pack and would not be opened up again for any stake.

***

He entered the room and looked quickly around, not really taking anything in. He was looking for Chris and nothing else. There was a deal to be done and that was it.

His cards would be firmly laid out on the table, no jokers, no wild cards, no nothing. The stakes may be high, they may be raised but until he started playing the game he did not know what would be fully expected of him. Only the outcome was known and that is what he was playing for.

He saw Chris from across the room. There were a lot of occupied tables, lots of inmates and visitors. Chris raised his hand to about half mast to help him find him quicker. He sat down in front of him, their eyes met and the games began.

Chris dealt the first card upwards...

His visitor agreed to help. He agreed to do whatever he needed to do to get what he wanted.

He dealt his next card upwards...

He told Chris exactly what he wanted to get out of this little business deal. Chris agreed to his terms and conditions.

The next card was dealt face down...

Chris leaned forward and quietly whispered a name in his ear. His visitor said nothing and barely even nodded as a response, but he understood.

The next card was dealt face down too...

"This evening," whispered Chris, "just before 'The Black Queen' is on, I will let you know what you have to do."

He looked back at Chris confused.

How?

Chris read his mind.

"Don't worry about that," he said. "I will let you know."

And with that, Chris stood up, pushed his chair under the table and headed back towards his cell.

The visit was short but it was far from sweet.

Guaranteed though, somebody was destined to fall.

Somebody was destined to die.

Q♥ CHAPTER 34 Q♥

The day after Bonfire night

Mark (AKA Connie) stood facing The Maniac. His legs were trembling so much that he was worried that the floor boards may start creaking from the tremors he was creating.

He needed to speak but words failed to pour out of him.

What was he scared of?

This room? This house? This street? The Northern Territory? The Maniac?

His past?

His dark and not so distant past catching up with him and changing his present and his future?

Yes, that was it. Mark was fighting for his life and he would have to play all his Aces to win his life back.

"Well, Kid, what do you want?" asked The Maniac. "Why are you here?"

Mark knew he needed to speak. He wouldn't be given long for The Maniac was a very busy man and this would be his only chance. "It's about Tequila," he finally explained.

"The drink or the drag queen bitch?"

At that moment, it could have been about both.

"The drag queen bitch," Mark replied.

"What about him, her, it?"

The Maniac's mood was just very slightly beginning to change even just at the thought of it. Mark could sense it happening. They had all seen this shift in behaviour before, they knew what might follow. First of all, the teeth began to grit together, the eyes then closed up and the fists began to clench.

Mark was not given enough time to respond. "What about it?" The Maniac demanded to know once more.

"The police raid on The Queen's Legs cabaret bar, I presume that was all your doing?"

Of course, it was" replied The Maniac, proudly smiling to himself. "I got that naff, little drag queen arrested. I wish I could have seen her face though. I hear she was dragged off the stage in front of everyone; how humiliating for it."

"But why?"

"Oh come on, you know I love to dish out my little warnings, Mark."

"And has there been anything else?"

"Oh just a few little cut and paste letters. It keeps the Heavies busy when there's not a lot going on. We even sent one to that other drag queen too. Ha, that was funny. Actually, we have no problem with that one at all, but she needs to know how bloody crap she is.

"Now what was it we said to Tequila? Oh yes, it was something like: Enjoy your performance; you never know when it might be your last."

Mark didn't know about the letters, but it was not entirely a surprise to him. Thinking about it, it made sense now because when he was stalking people from afar through social media, Wendy had posted about a delightful fan letter she had received.

Knowing her and knowing her delusion, a death threat of sorts would most definitely have been misinterpreted as an acknowledgment of appreciation.

"Oh, how we laughed, Mark," he continued to say. "You would have laughed too. I presume he received it safely. I presume they both did."

"I would have thought so," replied Mark, not prepared to share what he suspected.

The Maniac turned serious again. "Right, Kid, so what do you really want me to do?"

"Please back off Tequila. He's not a bad lad underneath. He's just a bit up himself, that's all."

"He's just a bit thick, that's what he is."

"So will you please let him off?"

"No."

"Will you please do it for me; for old time's sakes?"

"No."

Mark was desperate. He didn't want to resort to playing his wild card but he felt he had very little choice left now. "How about if Connie was to come and pay you a little visit?" he suggested, feeling quite repulsed at just the very suggestion of it.

"No. I want Tequila. I don't want you. Not anymore. I never really wanted you anyway, I just wanted to get at Chris Randall, and you provided the perfect route in."

"What?"

"I have been after Chris Randall's territory for a long time. Yeah, he did okay out of it but I knew I could do a lot better. His mistake was letting idiots like Tequila sell them on for him."

"Honestly, Tequila really is a good lad."

"Tequila is fucking scum who sold some of those drugs on to my son. I don't care what anybody else does in this town, but my children do not have anything to do with any of it. The shit she sold him caused him to have a seizure. He could've died because of that stupid bitch."

"No, it was because of Chris Randall, remember? That's why we joined forces to get back at him."

"No. I have now decided it's because of her; that's what I remember."

"But if your son chose to buy them then the problem was already there. Tequila didn't start it; she just stupidly added further fuel to the problem."

214

The Maniac clearly did not like what he was hearing. "Right, I want you to go now before you say something really stupid. You're really starting to irritate me and I don't want to be pissed off by you, not whilst we still like each other."

Mark nodded. He knew it had all been a waste of time. He should have known it would be. He turned to leave but stopped and turned around when he was spoken to once more.

"Oh just one more thing," said The Maniac. "I am coming after Tequila and I will get her. But if you get in the way of that then believe me I will come after you instead."

Mark did believe him.

He left the building and the Northern Territory as quickly as he could. Damn it, he hadn't helped at all. It would probably have been better had he left it all alone.

And now, things would probably happen even quicker than they might have done beforehand.

Okay, so he needed to get to Tequila as quickly as he could to warn her of the dangers ahead, and he needed to break another of his life's affirmations.

He pulled out his mobile phone and swiped a few screens out of the way. And for no other reason than to know if they were ever ringing him, he scrolled through a list of people he vowed never to contact again.

He stopped on one particular name and rang their number.

Of course there was always a chance that they had changed their number or would not answer.

There was always a chance that they too had numbers in their phone so they also knew which calls to ignore. But Mark had understandably changed his number since fleeing this town and the number would come up as unknown on the other end.

Would they answer?

Would they not?

It began to ring.

When it hadn't been answered by the fourth ring, Mark looked quickly at his watch to check the time. Surely they would be awake and up and at it by now?

Hmmmm, should he leave a message or not? Probably best to try again in a while, but this was important and he needed to speak to the other person urgently.

It rang several more times and then thankfully it was answered.

He began to plead his case. "Hi, it's me Mark ... Yes, Connie. Well, Connie was as is the case now, but that's all irrelevant... What do I want? Okay, I actually need a massive favour; a really, really massive favour. The trouble is, you're probably not going to like doing it one bit. But for old time's sakes, will you please help me? ..."

And as he continued to speak, what Mark didn't realise is that one of the Heavies had been sent to follow him.

And as he continued to speak, what Mark didn't realise is that the Heavy was within clear hearing distance and would be able to give The Maniac a full rundown of events.

And what Mark didn't realise is that he was now in grave danger too.

At April Showers' psychic evening, Wendy couldn't help but stop and talk into the TV cameras every time she passed one.

"I am best friends with Miss April Showers, you know. Isn't she a love?"

She wobbled over to another camera. "Me and Miss April Showers are real bosom buddies. In fact, I'm wearing her padded bra right now. But she doesn't know that, so best not tell her."

She turned to face quite a stressed young person who was holding a clipboard and looking around for somebody who clearly wasn't there.

"Have you met Miss April Showers?" Wendy asked him. "She's almost as famous as I am. She's the Psychic Drag Queen, don't you know? Are you part of the production crew? Are you looking for her? Would you like me to pop backstage and hurry her along? We're proper gal pals, don't you know?"

And with that she finally wandered over to the buffet table to help herself to just the tiniest morsel of just about everything that would fit onto her plate.

"We'll probably both do a season together in Benidorm," she continued to say to anybody who was listening. "How simply divine for me! Well, for her mostly, wouldn't you agree? After all, I have headlined the Divas cabaret show, so I know what I am doing. Only once though, but I reckon Chris will want me on board full time now. Do you know Chris? He's very handsome and he's going to be my fiancé. Would you like to come to the wedding?"

Yes, that evening at April Showers' psychic event, Wendy was unstoppable. In fact, the bullshit, like the name-dropping, was simply oozing out of every pore; even more so than normal.

This evening was happening just a week or so after she had been on the Mrs Seavers Show and had performed her headlining show at Divas cabaret bar, and naturally she felt invincible; she felt like a TV star.

And it didn't matter that she had been utterly awful and Chris had had her pulled off the stage, because nobody there knew her from Adam or rather Eve and all they knew is what Wendy repeatedly told them.

And what Wendy told them tended to be glitter sprayed and covered in pretty, pink gingham trim.

And just to add one further cherry on top of her over-sized dragged up trifle she had also become 'best friends' with April Showers after their respective performances on the Mrs Seavers Show too.

Except April didn't really know that, for they hadn't actually met; although in the mind of Wendy, they had, and in the ears of anyone she told, they had.

But in all honestly, all that had happened so far was a quick knock on April's dressing room door after the Mrs Seavers Show, to which Wendy had then run away from nervously when the semi-famous person who was sometimes on TV had appeared there to see who was knocking them up.

In fact, April didn't even know her name, and of course Wendy had been edited out of the actual version of the show that was aired so there was no evidence of her ever having been there anyway.

But to Wendy, just that glance at April, that brief encounter had been more than enough. And to April, all she knew is that some blown up *weeble* with the wrong coloured lipstick was warming up the audience for her.

April had recently been receiving some bad media attention, particularly for some over-fetched predictions that never actually happened, and she couldn't afford a further glitch in her psychic career, and besides what harm could it possibly do if someone had taken it upon themselves to turn up that evening and lie about their friendship.

Actually, in some ways it was rather quite flattering. All the best people are cursed with weird, deluded stalkers and now she had one too.

And that evening, Wendy had even padded out her hips to resemble April's trademark hour-glass figure and be just like her.

Well, not so much padded out her hips but more so shoved a hot-water bottle up each side of her dress which she couldn't resist telling somebody by the quiche that it had once belonged to a really famous Hollywood actress with a massive backside.

Unfortunately, she had not used the same sized hot water bottles, so rest assured, her hips were not even remotely symmetrical, but people like Wendy, just couldn't be told and in her eyes, she had yet again achieved perfection with her latest look.

And what else can be expected when her size zero reflection giggles back at her and is almost as deluded as she is.

Now that evening, Wendy and April were not the only drag queens there and Wendy had spotted Miss Jet Black immediately, but had purposefully avoided her because she was just too beautiful to approach.

And even the supreme champion of delusion had to draw the line of realism somewhere.

Perhaps if she had paid more attention, she would have realised that their paths had already crossed at Divas cabaret bar, but that had gone by the way. As, it would seem, had Wendy's manners when April turned up to face her audience and give her first reading of the night.

"Me first! Me first! Me first!" she had screamed, pushing many of the others out of the way.

And before anybody could even begin to protest or push back, Wendy had plonked herself down on the seat opposite April and insisted on being told everything that the spirit world needed to tell her, particularly in the areas of fame and fortune, and love and romance.

And April was most taken aback by this.

She knew she had to perform well that evening, for all eyes and TV cameras were on her, but Wendy was not the one she had pre-arranged to be sitting in front of her, what with her larger than life personality demanding all the attention.

No, this would never do. But what could she do? It was all on her and Wendy now.

April could feel the sweat forming under the lining of her wig. Soon it would start to trickle down her face and sting her eyes. Her makeup would start to streak; this could be a disaster.

Wendy should not be sitting there. The one who should have been sitting there, in front of her, had been pushed to the ground with heel imprints across their back, from top to bottom.

But April was now forced to play the cards dealt to her. For when all was said and done, she was actually a charlatan and had made a nice career out of deceiving people.

Sometimes she could make reasonable attempts at working somebody out. Generally there were money worries, lost love or loneliness. The younger tended to want to know about their careers or travel. These situations were all quite easy to manipulate.

The lonely ones in particular tended to talk more than April did. All she had to do was offer a few chosen words of reassurance, a careful nod of the head and occasionally a message that their loved ones were with them. This usually gave them enough hope and belief to tell others how good the Psychic Drag Queen was without really allowing any time to contemplate what had or hadn't been said.

In a way, one Miss April Showers had built up her career just from listening and understanding; more of a counsellor than a psychic, but perhaps now she deserved to be exposed.

Perhaps it was time somebody stood up and shamed her.

As Wendy was waiting for the reading to begin, across the room, April noticed Miss Jet Black immediately. She sensed her stare on her and you didn't have to be psychic or intuitive to know she was being targeted in some way.

April could feel the sweat dripping down her face and across her shoulders and down her back.

She felt like she was next in line to fall and this was her doomsday.

She wanted to tear her wig off as she felt like this gorgeous drag queen in the crowd with the jet black hair was about to take everything from her, drain her of all her energy and bleed her dry in whatever way she was able to.

She could feel the hairs on her arms stand on end, which for a drag queen was never a good look.

She could also sense Wendy staring back at her impatiently; waiting for all manner of affirmations and predictions about becoming an international superstar, bathing in bank notes and being bombarded by scrummy dream boats and petticoats.

April couldn't help but stare at Jet, she wondered if she would be able to take from her what she had set out to achieve.

Of course she knew she could. It felt like if anybody had something and she wanted it, it would be hers.

Was she here to expose her, is that what this was all about?

Regardless of the circumstances, it was all up for grabs. And based on her posture, her presence and that stare, there wouldn't be much left by the time she had had her fill, and she looked ravenous.

April Showers was definitely her next victim, but why?

April continued to ignore Wendy and to stare at Jet. She also ignored the faces of the crowd who were also waiting impatiently for her to begin.

She was very striking to look at; far too beautiful to be there that night in amongst all the desperation and wanton hopefuls.

She was drinking something neat from a small glass. It was a clear liquid. It might have been water, but unlikely. It was probably gin or white rum. Maybe it was vodka.

She watched her take a sip and then another. She put it down, unfinished and never touched it again. Maybe she needed a clear head. All this time though, her gaze never broke from its target.

She seemed invincible like a wrecking ball.

April stopped and reached for the glass of water in front of her. Deep inside, she was terrified, but impressed with herself that she seemed to be holding her nerve. She sensed it was the right way to be.

What else could she do?

She stared back at Wendy who was still sitting opposite her.

"Predictions please," it hollered back at her.

April knew she needed to do or say something for it had been too long now without anything being said.

It wasn't just Wendy who was waiting, it was a whole open room, so many others were watching, waiting to see if there was any point hanging around to find out what their futures held; all waiting to see if the Psychic Drag Queen was as good or perhaps as bad as they had recently heard.

April could see Jet slowly meandering toward her. Perhaps she wanted a reading. It was definitely a now or never situation, and something had to happen and now, right now.

And that's when she turned back to Wendy and lost absolute focus. That's when she lost control and she turned the thoughts and fears created by the stunning one towards the scruffy queen in front of her.

"You're just a bloody nightmare, aren't you?" April said. "Sucking the life and soul out of everything like an energy vampire. I bet everyone dreads you coming into the room. Why are you even here? Nobody wants you here. You're just delusional if you think people care."

There were gasps of horror and surprise from all those around, and even Miss Jet Black herself took a backward step and disappeared quickly into the background, hidden temporarily by the shock of others.

Whatever she had planned to do was temporarily aborted with immediate effect.

Maybe it was because of what had happened or maybe it was because she recognised Wendy close up, but either way, her work there was not yet done.

"I can't do this anymore," muttered April quietly to herself, and barely anyone heard her. "I can't keep on with this charade."

All they heard was Wendy's response.

"How dare you," she responded to April, standing up and towering over the diminishing drag queen in front of her. "Everything you have said is a complete lie and I was your best friend too. I am not delusional, but you clearly are. Now consider our friendship well and truly over. I shall go back to being best friends with Miss Sugar Daddy; at least she is who she says she is. She is one hundred percent not a fake."

And with that, Wendy stood up and marched off with her head held high and her heels buckling inwards, not knowing in the slightest that Miss Sugar Daddy was also not who she claimed to be.

And all April could do was watch her leave until she was lost out of sight amongst the disappointed crowd that all had something to say about the situation and who all wanted refunds immediately.

There was no point continuing now; the truth was out. There could be no turning back now, not from this.

And it was most unlikely that anybody would ever trust her to make a prediction ever again.

And soon enough, April was more or less alone in the room as most people had already made their way back out of the door and to the front desk to complain.

There was little point in them hanging around any longer; there would be no predictions for them and if there was who would ever believe them now?

The TV cameras were turned off. They would be removed soon enough. The production crew had disappeared from sight too.

This was going to be the worst media exposure she had ever received, and it had all been filmed too.

Her career as a drag queen and a psychic was over.

And as she sat there, she noticed an application form in front of her for a new TV drag queen reality show.

And as she sat there, she noticed the stunning drag queen with the jet black hair was watching her from the distance.

Had she left this application form for her?

Is that what her intentions had been all along?

It had felt as though a much stronger force had been at play, but now she would never know.

A new reality TV show for drag queens that would be filmed and aired that summer! Yes, that might be quite a fun new challenge to undertake.

Perhaps this was just what she needed. She was no longer going to be deemed a psychic but she could try to revive a career as just a drag queen and a bloody good one too.

Maybe she could apply, be selected and wow everybody once more with her 'psychic ability' in front of different TV cameras and a different audience.

This unfortunate incident and those that had led up to this day would all just become a thing of the past.

All she needed now was a plan on how she could do this and make people believe in her 'psychic abilities' once again.

She could be one of the ten drag queens chosen, couldn't she?

Yes, she would like that very much.

Q💔 CHAPTER 36 Q💔

Bonfire night

Jay shook himself, zipped back up his trousers and washed his hands thoroughly before placing them under the hand drier.

He opened the toilet door and stepped back into The Queens Leg's cabaret bar. Oliver was standing right there with his hand up against the cellar door.

Their eyes momentarily met.

Oliver looked away immediately, pushed open the cellar door firmly and went inside. The door closed very slowly behind him.

Almost everybody had left the venue to go out onto the street to watch the fireworks, and those that were still in there were quickly leaving.

In just a matter of a few seconds, he was standing all alone in there with Wayne at the bar.

And as there was nobody else in there in that moment, it seemed like the perfect opportunity to buy himself a drink. "I'll have a pint of lager please."

"Oliver has just gone down into the cellar to change the barrel," explained Wayne. "He'll probably be a while yet because he can't do it; maybe a bottle instead?"

"I'll have a pint of bitter instead then," replied Jay, beckoning his head towards a different beer pump.

Wayne nodded, picked up a pint glass and quickly poured the drink. "That'll be three pounds eighty," he said.

Jay passed over a five pound note and waited for his change. "Thank you," he replied, shoving the loose coins into his jeans pocket without checking them.

"Are you going out to watch the firework display?" Wayne asked. "Because I would like to see it too, but I can't if you stay in here."

"Sure, I'll go out and watch them," replied Jay.

Wayne locked the till, pocketed the key and walked around the bar.

They both left the venue together and quickly lost each other in the crowd that had formed outside.

Jay was thankful for that as he did not have any intention of standing together, side by side, making small talk about the pretty colours, the slightly supernatural sounding noises that screamed out of each and every firework, how they liked rockets best and how Catherine Wheel would be a great name for a drag queen.

Literally right after the first rocket went up and exploded into a blaze of reds and greens, Jay turned away and slipped back into the pub.

Nobody saw him go in as all their focus was on the fireworks; barely anybody had even noticed he was there.

His eyes immediately went straight to the cellar door. It was no longer closed, but it was slowly closing; very much in the same slow, clunky manner as it had done when Oliver had gone in there previously to change the barrel.

Maybe it was closing because Oliver had come out, but he was nowhere to be seen.

Not behind the bar and not in the toilets. Maybe he had gone backstage, but why?

Surely he wouldn't still be in the cellar? Not even if he didn't know how to change a barrel?

It had been a while.

Should he go down there too?

Standing at the top of the cellar steps he listened carefully but there was nothing to hear. It appeared to be deathly silent down there, except for the noise of fireworks outside.

Then there was something to hear, there were distant footsteps and they seemed to be heading right for the stone steps. In a moment they would be at the door and whoever it was would know he was there; trying to solve a mystery that may or may not even exist.

Jay dashed away, back out onto the street and quickly lost himself in the crowd out there, whilst still managing to keep an eye on what was happening on the inside through the pub windows.

If it was Oliver, he didn't want him to know that he had been in there spying on him.

But it wasn't Oliver who came out of the cellar and suddenly Jay was concerned.

Maybe there was a mystery to unpick, after all.

So, where the Hell was Oliver?

For the rest of that evening, unlike the others, he did not leave early. He sat on a seat opposite the bar and nursed his pint until closing time.

Just sitting there and watching there and waiting there.

Waiting for any opportunity to go down into those cellars and investigate what was going on for himself.

Even if it meant he would have to spend the night down there.

Even if it meant he would not possibly get any sleep until the next day.

The day after Bonfire night

Mark (AKA Connie) finally returned to East Green Street. And this was yet another one of those places that he had relentlessly vowed he would never return to.

Chris Randall had lived nearby and Mark had often staggered down this way, in full drag and through the darkness of the night, for his next much-needed fix or to pass on messages from The Maniac.

And, just for one night only, to insist on being given the lead in the Divas cabaret show.

This was all at a time when he had been winning the game of life and had taken full advantage of the unexpected opportunities that seemed to come his way.

He hoped he would soon and quickly return to those feelings of empowerment because at that moment he felt he was losing himself once more.

And that really was the one place he vowed he would absolutely never return to.

This time, he had come to The Queen's Legs cabaret bar to find Miss Tequila ShockingBird and then he would be able to leave.

He stood outside to admire the changes, but they were few and far between.

Admittedly, the name over the door was different: Martin Taylor-Smith 'licensed to get people intoxicated and find Wendy WolfWhistle much more desirable whilst under the influence' and of course the pub name was different too, but that was about it.

...The legacy of Divas will one day rise again
But the people and the name
And the place won't be the same
And the nightmares that return will find their pain...

He pushed open the door and stepped inside to see some more notable changes. It was almost early evening by now and not yet that busy, but he hadn't expected it to be rammed to the rafters at that time.

It definitely looked better inside even though there were still very clear remnants of the former pub, for example the slight odour of chips and dog trumps, but that could just have been the smell of the lingering afternoon punters. The stage was still situated at the far end, albeit much grander than the previous one which had once hosted the meat raffle and the occasional game of bingo which he had never played.

But all in all, it was definitely better than it had been, and if Mark was still a local and his past and present had both been quite different, he would probably be quite excited that this new drag queen pub existed for his entertainment.

One thing that hadn't changed though was the old bar; it still stood in exactly the same place and behind the bar still stood Wayne the stain.

Now it felt like the old days again.

Mark cringed slightly to see his slightly miserable face, but who wouldn't be miserable

234

if they had stood behind that bar for years on end desperately trying to make ends meet.

It was unlikely that Wayne would recognise him as Mark, for their paths as Wayne and Mark had never crossed. But as Connie, well, that was almost guaranteed to instigate some sort of reunion.

But never as Mark.

Quite determined and with his eye on the bigger picture, Mark walked over to him and asked if James (AKA Tequila) was about. He kept it cool and breezy so as not to bring untoward attention to himself. Wayne acknowledged that he was about somewhere and proceeded to head backstage; informing the chosen one that somebody had come to see him.

He quickly returned to the bar area and back to his own life and dreams... First of all, he would get out of that awful and badly-lit studio flat that had once accommodated Wendy WolfWhistle, and then he would...

But James came out into the pub area and as Wayne gestured him towards the place where Mark was patiently standing, his dreams were momentarily forgotten, and as he moved to the end of the bar to serve yet another hopeful person who too had dreams that often went unheard, he felt he would never be free of this.

"And what do you want, bitch?" James demanded to know the moment he laid eyes on him.

And this instantly made the early evening much more interesting for the few punters who were in there drinking and, up until that point, had probably been slightly bored as they sat there staring at their pints.

But this was very much the response that Mark had expected to receive and he had braced himself for the impact.

Thank goodness it was not likely that James or anybody else for that matter knew he had been linked to the Divas fire, otherwise he would never break his way through and enter James's trust.

"Can we talk?" Mark hopefully asked. "It's important, really important."

"If you're after the lead in the show, well you can just piss right off now," responded James. "This is my show and I am the lead act."

"I thought Wendy was," replied Mark quite flippantly as that is what was implied on social media – on Wendy's profile, of course.

"Er... No. It's very much me. And I'm way better than you ever were. I kill it out there but when you had your chance, you just murdered it."

And Mark could not disagree with that.

James was clearly growing bored off this discussion and turned to walk away backstage. He was the top drag queen there and he didn't want anybody else upsetting his apple cart; especially has-beens from a different time and place who no longer had room in his life.

And who no longer even had a frock to their name.

"No listen," replied Mark, cheekily walking after him backstage and away from the prying eyes and ears within the pub area, "there's something we really have to sort out and quickly."

"Are you here to have sex with me?" asked James, "is that what this is about? Believe me, knowing where you have been or rather not knowing, the answer is no."

And once again, Mark could not disagree with that, but this banter was not getting them anywhere and time was not on any of their sides.

James had always been a slightly flaky character, always out of his depth and high maintenance and obviously very little had changed in that regard, except now he was the star of the show and that had clearly heightened his own self-worth and what he believed his public perception to be.

And good on him; it was what he had always wanted and now he was ruling the roost.

"Right, I have an evening performance to get ready for," announced Tequila, "and you are distracting my zen focus and my feng shooey as that Shimmy bird says. The door is that way. Make sure you never see this side of it again."

Mark knew he had just one last chance to engage James in discussion.

He had to save him and he could now only think of just one more thing to say that might work. "Enjoy your performance," he said, "you never know when it might be your last."

And that really seemed to work.

James's face dropped slightly when he heard those words as nobody knew about that letter. "Bitch, did you send me that?" he squealed.

"No, I didn't," he responded. "The Maniac did."

"The Maniac? And who's that when he's at home in his wife's clothes?"

"He is a really terrifying man who is after you."

"And why would he be after me?" scorned James.

"Look, this is really serious," advised Mark, concerned that James did not believe a word he was saying. "Can we talk somewhere privately?"

James nodded. Perhaps if he had his say then he might go away. "If we have to do this then you'd better come upstairs to my room," he replied, leading the way there. "But just so you know, I'm still not having sex with you, no matter how much you might want to."

"Fair enough," replied Mark, humouring him once again.

Mark was taken up some stairs and into the living quarters above the pub which James insisted on telling him all about en route.

But the truth is Mark already knew the way there and the layout. He had already been up there a few times beforehand with Wayne when he had had a wallet full of spare twenties.

Fortunately, James took him to a doorway and into a room that he had never been into before. It was James's bedroom and it was tiny.

"So where have you been since Divas came crashing down then?" asked James.

"Never mind that now," replied Mark, who didn't want anybody to know where he had been or where he was heading back to; even if he needed to build that wall of trust around them both. "How have you been?"

"I don't know if you know," he replied, "but I was in hospital for a while after the fire but look at me now. I am the phoenix that rose from the ashes."

Mark smiled. Yes, he did know that but he wasn't about to admit that he had been stalking him through social media from a distance.

"So... This Maniac?" questioned James, "and the letter too?"

"What is it all about?"

James nodded. Understandably he didn't have a clue what was going on, but he just suddenly felt that he had to believe Mark who had obviously gone out of his way to resurface after all these months.

For once in his life, James felt he should stop and listen and be the less dominating individual who thought they knew everything but literally never answered a single question when asked anything.

"The Maniac is after you," explained Mark. He's been biding his time; waiting for the trail to go cold, that's what these people do, they sit and wait before they destroy their prey. And if he knew I was here telling you this, he would be after me too."

"Why?"

"It's a very long story," replied Mark, and he began from the very beginning, reiterating in parts things that James already knew and adding new ventures along the way until he reached the point where they were both sitting there together in that tiny bedroom fearing for their lives.

Naturally Mark omitted some things.

Things that James didn't need to know about; more so about his own personal misdemeanours but things that might have broken the circle of trust in which they now both sat.

The key points were as follows:

1. When Tequila joined Divas she replaced Miss Crystal Champagne who, up until that point, had no intention of leaving until Chris Randall made her go.

No, she is not The Maniac, Mark explained.

Nor is Chris Randall, Mark further explained.

2. Chris asked Tequila to sell drugs on for him, probably to get what she wanted like being the lead in the Divas cabaret show which she didn't get.

James agreed that that had been his recollection of the situation too. He had been promised the lead in the show and everyone else bar him had been given the chance to do that, even flippin' Wendy WolfWhistle (momentarily).

3. Tequila, without intention, had sold drugs to The Maniac's son which was a massive mistake.

James looked quite panicked by this. He had always regretted selling on those drugs and even more so now. He now also regretted not heeding the advice provided at the time by both Mark (Connie Lingus as he was then) and Tittie Mansag.

Of course, if he had known that there were people in the background with names like The Maniac then he would have thought twice about it all, but he had not been handed an idiots guide to selling drugs. Clearly he wasn't as streetwise back then as he had always perceived himself to be.

4. The Maniac came after Chris Randall for drug-related matters and debts spiralling out of control and he had had Divas burnt down as a result of it.

Naturally, Mark continued to exclude his own involvement in any part of it. And if James ever had the bright spark to question how he and The Maniac knew each other then he would have to cross that bridge but he didn't think that he would be asked as James was really not that bright.

And James didn't ask. He was already thinking about himself, just as Mark knew he would be. He was thinking about his own spiralling debts that he was still hiding from and of course every thought now led him back to his growing fears about The Maniac.

The Maniac - a man he had never met and never even knew existed until now. And he was after him.

Oh dear, James felt he was too young and too pretty to be broken by such a person.

It never dawned on him at any point that any of this could have been a lie, for he trusted Mark explicitly.

5. The Maniac has been biding his time but warnings have been sent; the police raid on opening night and the cut and paste letter. They were warnings not to be ignored and James had been ignoring them. This meant time was running out.

Mark believed he knew what James was thinking. He should do, he had intentionally led him in that direction. "We have to get you out of here," he said.

"But I have nowhere to go," replied James sadly.

And it was said sadly because one stupid mistake had led him to this, but also because he feared that this was the end of his reign as the gorgeous and much loved Tequila

ShockingBird and the cabaret show that he had had so much input into.

But then again, he also knew Martin's secret and that it was actually Chris who owned The Queen's Legs and who only knew what future that path might hold for any of them.

"Don't worry, I have a plan in place for you," advised Mark reassuringly, and then he surprised both himself and James by putting his arms around him and hugging him and holding him close.

And then he finally felt some of the guilt release itself.

And then he finally felt the burden that clung so tightly to his back become slightly more bearable.

And then he finally felt that perhaps he wasn't such a bad person, after all.

But this was all about James...

And this needed to be all about James.

"Okay, what's the plan?" asked James releasing himself, although he had wanted to hold on for just that little bit longer as he had felt safe and warm being comforted by this familiar person with whom he had never given a chance to get to know before.

"Okay, this took some convincing but you remember I mentioned that other drag queen from Divas: Miss Crystal Champagne."

"The one that I, this bitch, replaced?"

Mark nodded for James had been that bitch. "She is living out in Gran Canaria now. She runs a drag queen bar out there. She has said you can go out there and work for her."

"Gran Canaria?" replied James slightly stunned. "Yikes, that's scary."

"But much safer."

"I know," replied James, suddenly overcome with emotion. "It's tempting, I must admit. And she is okay with me going out there, if I wanted to?"

"She is, and once I told her how good you are and how committed you are to drag, she agreed to let bygones be bygones. Look, she worked with Chris long enough, we all did, and she knows how he operates."

"Okay, well, that's good."

"In fact, she said you did her a massive favour by replacing her. She got away from Divas, away from Chris and took a chance and she's having a ball out there. Now it's time for you to take a chance too, James."

"But I'm scared."

"What, fearless Tequila is scared of doing something fantastic like this?"

"No, she isn't but James is scared to do something like this," he explained anxiously.

Mark tried to reassure him. "You'll be okay out there with Crystal, she'll look after you."

"I haven't got any money to buy a plane ticket and where would I live?"

"Don't worry about that, I have money you can have. And as for where you'll live, you will stay with Crystal in the short-term, and in the longer-term you'll get somewhere.

"Apparently she lives in a gorgeous little apartment complex with a swimming pool and other British ex-pats. Something may come up for rent there. Just think, you could sun bathe everyday of the year."

"It does sound amazing," said James thoughtfully, "it really does. But I can't take your money as well; you have done enough for me already."

Mark felt that after the danger he had put them all in, this was barely the tip of the iceberg. "Okay, as we are being completely honest, would it help if you knew that it wasn't entirely my money that I would be giving to you?"

"What?"

"It's actually Chris's money, well it was his money; it's mine now. I call it compensation for my troubled past. Let's face it, he doesn't need it where he is, does he?"

"Oh my God!" shrieked James.

"Oh my God... what?"

"I'm going to Gran Canaria," he replied.

"You sure are. Right, we need to book you a plane ticket."

"Now?"

"You need to go ASAP."

"But what about Wendy?" asked James, suddenly taking an unanticipated chop at the family tree.

"Crystal only has room for you."

"But he's my Father and we have only just found each other again. I know he's a pain in the arse but even so."

"He can visit," replied Mark comfortingly. "And you never know, he may even come and live with you once you are settled. Gran Canaria is full of drag queen bars; he could get a job out there too. I don't know what doing but something."

"Yes, I suppose he could," agreed James thoughtfully. "Wow, I'm going to live in the sunshine."

"And you are okay with all of this?"

"Yes. Gosh, I just can't believe I'm actually going to do this. How fast is all this?"

"Right, just to be on the safe side, let's try and get you a ticket out of here tomorrow."

"Tomorrow, wow, okay. So what should I tell people?"

"Don't tell them anything. The less people know about this the better."

"My Father will be upset."

"Yes, he will be," agreed Mark, "but then he'll realise that he is the headlining star of the show."

And Mark's guilt lifted a little bit more as he realised that through the process of helping James he was making another person's dreams come true.

James laughed a little. "Yes, that will help ease the blow."

As Mark searched his phone for flights, he turned to James and said. "Do the show tonight, I'm sure everything will be okay, but do not leave this building until the taxi turns up to take you to the airport. The Maniac won't try anything with an audience."

"How do you know so much about him?" asked James.

Mark smiled and said the only thing that came to mind, which in theory wasn't far from the truth anyway. "He helped me bring down Chris Randall."

"He deserved it after what he did to everybody, especially you," replied James, and this time he showed some love back to the other person in the room.

"Right, how many cases will you need?"

"I will probably need three; one for my stuff and two for Tequila. Everything else can stay here."

Mark took out his wallet and inputted his credit card details. You do have a passport, don't you?"

"Of course. I'm always ready to go."

"Good, right I'll sort out your taxi and I'll need to make a bank transfer to your account too. The wonders of modern technology, eh?"

James smiled back at him.

"And Crystal will pick you up from the airport out there, so you won't have to worry about that either. Oh and you will have to change your drag queen name too."

"Why?"

"Modern technology may be wonderful, but you don't want anybody stalking Tequila through social media from afar, do you? You never know who might turn up."

"Okay," agreed James. "I suppose a reinvention is always a good thing. How about Miss Venus Flytrap?"

"Don't tell me anything. Now do you have any further questions before I go?"

"No," he replied, "I don't. No wait... I do have just one question."

"And what's that?"

"Where exactly is Gran Canaria?"

***

And as Mark left the pub, and James, and everything else that the building reminded him of, he felt pleased that he had been able to do this; even if it had meant returning to this god-forsaken town.

Soon James would be safe.

Soon Wendy would be the lead cabaret star of the show.

And soon he would be back to his own life on the south coast and he would be safe once more too.

Unfortunately, he was too pre-occupied in releasing his own guilt, building bridges and applauding his own successes that he continued to let his guard down without thinking about it.

He had made another fatal error where The Maniac was concerned.

Mark hadn't spotted the Heavy who had followed him from the Northern Territory who had heard him on his phone and was now sitting and waiting in The Queen's Legs, monitoring his every move.

The Heavy who would continue to report back to The Maniac and advise him that Mark had once more gone against his wishes.

Stick or twist?

Hmmm...

Who loses?

Q💔 CHAPTER 38 Q💔

Bonfire night

Jay watched as they cleaned the bar around him.

It was closing time but he was not the last one in there, for there were still a few last minute Larries hanging on for whatever came their way before they finally had to admit defeat and walk the short distance back to their homes.

Time was running out and he needed to get down into those cellars. He had a bad feeling about all of this and there was no denying that Oliver seemed to have disappeared into thin air. There was nowhere else he could be but still down there.

He watched the chubby, older man who usually compared the show take the till drawer with him to the back; so that was one of them out of the way.

The last few hangers-on gave up and left, some going straight home, some perhaps going to the takeaway on the next street, others going off somewhere to investigate a new club elsewhere or a new phone app that guaranteed immediate action.

The one they called Tequila was nowhere to be seen. She herself had made a u-turn backstage when a steaming hot bucket of soapy water had appeared, which Wayne picked up and headed into the men's toilets with.

That just left Wendy WolfWhistle who was collecting up beer mats and wiping down tables, and, although still in drag, was decidedly looking more Arthur than Barbara as her five o'clock shadow was already showing through, one of her oversized earrings was long gone and the ladder running up the back of her tights was more than enough to show off a cross-section of hair on her big, left man leg.

So it was just Jay and Wendy and from his experience of Wendy, he knew she could be easily distracted by a new hair scrunchie or a virtual gastric band. Unfortunately, he had neither, but perhaps the latter could be available if he could give a convincing performance.

He wisely chose not to go down the route of either option.

"You were great tonight," he said to her.

"Ahhh thank you," she replied. "Did you get the pelvic thrust I did just for you during the finale?"

Jay smiled back at her. She was harmless enough; deluded beyond the worst of them and probably a great person to have gone trick or treating with a few days earlier, but nice enough on the whole and harmless too.

"Would you like my autograph, Darling?" she asked, walking over to the bar area with a few empty glasses, which she then put down. "I'm sure I have some that I prepared somewhere around here; now where are they?"

She hobbled and wobbled around the bar and quickly searched around the till area, but turned to face Jay empty-handed. "Oh, I think

I must have left them in my dressing room and we're not allowed to leave the bar area unattended."

"I'm not going to steal anything if you want to dash off and get me one."

"Sorry, Martin is really strict about this."

"Well, that is a shame," replied Jay, "because I would love to have your autograph, especially after giving me such a soul shaking pelvic thrust during the finale."

"Well, perhaps I could find a pen and scribble it on the back of something. Maybe I could sign your man breast?"

"That might be nice," replied Jay, unsure how else to respond to that suggestion.

"Oh, here's a pen," said Wendy, spotting one behind a half filled bottle of dark rum. "Start unbuttoning your top. Hmmm, I'd better check it works. Where I used to be the lead cabaret star, in a lovely place called Divas, we used to have brochures. I was in the brochure, you know."

She turned back around to face him, whilst smiling as she recollected such memories. Unfortunately, she had told so many people that story over time that she now actually believed it had happened.

However, when she turned around, pen poised and somewhat slightly excited to be autographing a manly chest, he had gone.

She didn't notice that the cellar door was slowly closing, nor did she notice the noise of the steps he was so desperately trying to muffle as best as he could.

With a quick mutter of 'how rude was he' followed by the realisation that he was probably so in love with her that he couldn't bear to be alone with her for any longer, she walked around the bar and locked the doors on yet another fantastic night in The Queen's Legs.

Shame really, she thought to herself, as she picked up the last couple of empties, he was probably a lot closer to pulling her than he ever dreamt he could be.

Oh what the heck, she was his for the taking.

Down in the cellar, Jay tiptoed around looking for clues or evidence or anything that might indicate that some sort of misadventure had recently occurred down there, but everything looked as it should be. Not that he was in anyway an expert in knowing all about pub cellar layouts or indeed misadventures of any sorts; well, maybe a little with the latter but nothing too significant.

There was another door down there, but it was padlocked. What was behind it? Could Oliver be hidden behind there? He listened carefully but could not hear anything.

He knocked quietly as he did not want to disturb the world above, but the world above him and the world around him did not respond.

A few moments later, the cellar lights were turned off from above and Jay was plunged into absolute darkness. Suddenly, he felt very foolish for playing detective in a situation he knew very little about.

Yes, he must have made a mistake, a huge mistake and now here he was alone in these miserable, cold cellars in the dark and locked inside the pub for the night.

What an idiot.

Oh, this was ridiculous.

Oliver couldn't possibly be down there. Why would he be?

He must have left the pub ages ago, and he must have left unnoticed. He was probably home right now watching the television or getting ready for bed; just like he should be too.

But Jay was adamant that he had not seen him leave.

Maybe something else would come undone in the meantime; some new information; further evidence; a clue of some description.

And once more he was playing detective again.

He waited down there for ages until he felt comfortable there was nobody left in the cabaret bar and they had all retired to their living quarters for the night. He took his mobile phone out of his pocket and switched on a torch light.

The cellar looked even more eerie than it had done beforehand, although the small ray of light from his phone was a welcome relief.

He headed towards the steps and as he climbed up them as silently as he could, he hoped that the cellar door itself had not been locked. He didn't relish the thought of having to spend the night down there; it was bad enough as it was, without that too.

Thankfully the door opened and he stepped into the bar area.

He was very much alone.

He helped himself to a few bags of nuts, accidentally pulling the cardboard holder off the wall and damaging the packaging in the process so it couldn't be hung back up. He poured himself a drink and sat all alone at one of the empty bar stools contemplating what to do next.

He was trapped inside there for the night, and there was no denying that. He needed to try and sleep, but that seemed to be an unlikely possibility and where would he sleep anyway?

He also needed to be somewhere safe and out of the way when the pub opened.

Oh, this was a ridiculous.

All this just to find Oliver, who was nowhere to be found anyway.

***

It was a long and lonely night for Jay inside the pub and his mission had appeared to be pointless and unnecessary.

Riddled with hunger and exhaustion, he had no choice other than to head back into the cellar just before dawn broke and to wait patiently down there for the place to open so he could sneak back up there again.

It would be a long wait and he hoped he would not be found, although the time down there gave him longer to explore.

And there was still no noise from behind that padlocked door.

He had found a light switch and dared to switch it on; it would save his phone battery which wasn't far off being critically low. He needed the remaining power for any emergency that may come his way.

In time, he would attempt to sneak back upstairs.

In time he would be sitting at the bar having a drink before he could take a much needed sleep.

In time Oliver's Mother would come in and re-confirm his suspicions that Oliver was missing.

In time, he would watch her leave the pub and he would follow her down the street, quickly catching her up.

In time, he would explain to her who he really was and tell her all about his suspicions.

In time, he knew he would have to sneak back into those cellars again, somehow cut open that padlock and see what was hidden behind that door.

And now... a short intermission

"Hi there, I'm Miss Shimmy Shoo and you probably best know me from starring in 'The Black Queen'.

"Today, I'm going to tell you all about my fabulicious new unisex fragrance. It's pronounced *Shimmer* but spelt (S)him/her from the *Made by Shimmy Shoo* range.

"*Shimmer* for both the man in you and the woman you long to be; available in participating retailers now, whilst stocks last.

"*Shimmer!* Why have two bottles in your drag bag when just one bottle will more than shoo-fice."

The day after Bonfire night

....Oliver blinked, for the shift from darkness to light had temporarily distracted his vision.

There was definitely somebody standing there, staring back at him as he lay helplessly in this, what he could now see, was a small room made of bricks and cracked cement and mortis and most definitely still within the cellars.

He saw their silhouette first and then as he grew accustomed to the light, he began to see who it was.

Standing there at the door looking down at him was Jay.

"Shush," warned Jay to him, putting his index finger across his own lips to make the suggestion of silence. "I'm here to rescue you and your Mother is waiting outside."

Jay quickly released the bounds that held Oliver captive and helped him to his feet, but he was wobbly for he had not moved for many hours and he was embarrassed as he had soiled himself.

But Jay did not care for he had achieved what he had set out to do. He had promised Oliver's Mother he would find her son and he had.

Jay texted her to let her know she had found him in the hidden underworld beneath The Queen's Legs cabaret bar. There was currently no signal, but as they moved back into civilisation the signal would grow strong and the message would be sent.

The police had been alerted by Oliver's Mother as soon as she had suspected he had disappeared, but Oliver was an adult and he hadn't been missing for long enough; besides he had apparently walked out of his job and had not been seen for a number of hours since then.

Oliver had not yet been considered as high risk, but given his recent past on East Green Street, he should have been.

"Do you know who did this to you?" Jay whispered, as he led him through the door that had held him prisoner and into the main cellar where Oliver had been trying to change a barrel the evening before.

"Can we talk outside?" replied Oliver huskily, for he was very thirsty and the insides of his throat felt as though they were stuck together.

"Of course," replied Jay and led him towards the stone steps that would lead them both safely out of there.

All Jay wanted was for Oliver to know that he could trust him. And hopefully that is what Oliver was doing; that he did trust him to help him through this traumatic ordeal.

Just who had wanted to do this to Oliver?

Who had dragged him to his Hell and held him prisoner; possibly to die of thirst or starvation or for the cold winter temperatures to take him first?

Seriously, who would want Oliver to die?

At the top of the stone steps, Jay forced open the door that led into the pub with such unexpected force that it slammed hard and suddenly all eyes were on him; even more so when Oliver appeared at his side, looking as dreadful as he was.

"What were you doing down there?" Martin demanded to know. Then he saw Oliver and silenced himself.

Oliver paid no attention to the startled and disturbed faces that stared back at him; he focussed solely on reaching the door in front of him that led the way back out to East Green Street and to his freedom.

He just needed to get out of there and back into the open space without glimpsing a single surprised look or without paying any attention to a single whisper about him.

He knew they would all talk about him and what they thought might have happened to him and had he really pissed himself, but as long as they waited until he was out of there, he really didn't care what they said for he couldn't stop the inevitable.

He had no control over the action and behaviours of others.

He was his own priority right now, and he kept focussing on getting himself through the door.

Oliver felt safe and comfortable with his arm around Jay; he suddenly felt like a comfortable stranger to him and, for a moment, just for a moment, he held him tighter than he had held anybody else since he had watched Jake slip away at the roadside.

Jay held open the door and led Oliver away from them all. Outside his Mother was already running down the street towards him, with tears in her eyes, and then Oliver had tears in his eyes too when he saw her.

And Jay tried to let go of him so they could hold each other, but Oliver's Mother wrapped her arms tightly around them both in gratitude and love.

This brave young man had saved her son's life. Thank goodness this decent person was in his life and looking after his welfare.

The stranger who had sat patiently and waited had turned out to be good, after all.

"We need to get you to the police station right now," said his Mother. "They need to find whoever did this to you and bolt him to the ceiling by his testicles."

"Yes, we do," agreed Oliver, as that was another step in the process to putting this all behind him.

"Do you know who did to you?" asked Jay once more. Now Oliver was in a safe zone with both himself and his Mother, he may want to speak more openly about what had happened.

"Do you mind if I just tell the police all about it?" requested Oliver. "I don't want to keep repeating myself."

"But you do know who did this to you, don't you?" asked Jay.

"Yes," replied Oliver, "I do know. I know exactly who did this to me."

And he just couldn't believe who it was.

Q💔 CHAPTER 40 Q💔

The day after Bonfire night

Mark (AKA Connie) was feeling isolated and trapped inside his hotel room.

He had completed what he had set out to do, or at least he hoped he had, and tomorrow he would be out of this town where soon nobody would probably even give him a second thought.

But tonight he felt enclosed within the four walls of his hotel room where many a person had come and gone and many more were yet to arrive for whatever reasons they had to be in this town.

A town where he would never be deemed a local man again.

He slipped into his comfortable jeans, a t-shirt and a thick black jumper for the November evening sky was star-filled and unbearably cold with a pending frost.

He put on his jacket, looked around the small, over-priced room where the furnishings and interiors almost all matched and closed the door tightly behind him.

He absolutely couldn't wait to leave, and had the journey home been manageable that evening, then he would already be on his way. Still the morning was only one night's sleep away and then he would well and truly be out of this place... forever.

He took the stairs down to the reception area and smiled politely at a couple coming in as he did so.

He didn't stop to make small-talk with them.

In all honesty, he couldn't care less whether they were having a lovely stay or not and he certainly didn't care to hear that their towels may not have been changed or their tea and coffee sachets had not been replenished.

He was a loner; he didn't need anybody anymore and he in no way wanted anybody to know him. Maybe in time he would open up about the new him, but never about who he had been, what he had done and what he had run away from.

Mark couldn't face going outside, but he really didn't want to be in his hotel room either nor did he want to be away from the safety of it.

Perhaps a quick drink in the hotel bar would help and a snack too, followed by chill-down time, an early night and away after breakfast.

Maybe even before breakfast.

Yes, that was the plan!

Well, for a few minutes anyway...

The bar was empty and Mark had barely taken a sip from his lager glass or a bite of his sandwich when he came into the bar area too.

Perhaps he was staying at this hotel too?

Mark recognised him straightaway.

He had a much-shorter haircut from how he once had and he looked quite tired around the eyes although a good night's sleep would soon sort that out.

There was absolutely no denying who it was and he was very surprised to see him there for it just didn't seem possible that he would be, but Mark was not in any position to judge anybody's past or reasoning.

The Arrival ordered a drink and looked around the empty bar. He seemed to instantly zoom in on Mark.

He walked over to him. "Do you mind if I join you?"

Mark nodded. "Sure," he said, although he didn't really want him there.

"Are you staying here too?"

Mark nodded again.

"It's not the best hotel, is it?" The Arrival continued to say. "Still it'll do for a night or two."

Mark nodded once more and wondered how long he would be able to get away with engaging in conversation with this person for, without really engaging with him in anyway. "It could be worse," he finally said.

It could be a lot better too. Still, it was the only hotel in town bar for a few bed and breakfasts here and there, and nosey old landladies rarely seemed to guarantee privacy or anonymity which they both definitely needed.

The Arrival leaned over and whispered near to Mark's ear. He was very careful not to disturb his personal space, but he needed to ask him something. Mark listened carefully, unsure of what he would hear.

Mark reiterated what he thought he had heard and told him what he wanted to know.

The Arrival nodded his appreciation and then took a sip from his drink; it all seemed very secret society. He didn't know how long he would be there drinking for, nor how long the person in front of him would be there for either. But he had learnt what he needed to know and help was on his side.

Mark looked back at him and longed once more for the peace and quiet he had craved that evening.

Oh why had he suddenly become involved in this?

Why was this person in front of him so familiar but yet also an absolute stranger?

Why did he have a feeling that slipping away silently after or even before breakfast was no longer an option?

Why did he have such a bad feeling, yet again?

Oh crap, here we go again... East Green Street!

***

The next morning, Mark arose early and headed towards East Green Street.

He intended to wait for The Arrival, make sure there were no problems and then he would be on his way again. Then he could grab his belongings, check out and be on his way once more.

Hopefully there would be no problem.

Hopefully this was all just down to his guilt and regret playing chopsticks on his heart strings, but he needed to know. He needed to know that everybody was safe, just once more before he left.

It was only one more thing to do and then he would be free of this god-forsaken town once and for all.

But maybe this god-forsaken town had other ideas for him. They had always had a love/hate relationship, mostly hate.

Maybe this god-forsaken town would have the last word.

The day after Bonfire night

It was very late in the evening when Oliver, Jay and his Mother returned to Oliver's (and Jay's) apartment block.

The statements had been taken, the details had been logged and the investigations to find the guilty party had begun.

Finally, Oliver was deemed to be a high risk case.

Finally, Oliver could shower, change into clean clothes and eat something.

His Mother made them all a hearty but simple meal, as Oliver did not have a lot of groceries in. Both young men wolfed down their food as though they hadn't eaten for days, which wasn't too far from the truth anyway.

Oliver was exhausted, Jay was exhausted and his Mother was exhausted; the adrenaline had been high and the emotions were high too.

"Right, you both need to get some sleep now," said his Mother.

Oliver nodded. "I'll be okay now, I promise."

"I have heard that one before," she replied.

"I can stay here with him," suggested Jay. "I'm happy to sleep on the settee; it's not a problem at all."

"Are you sure?" asked Oliver's Mother. "You won't have any of your things with you."

"I actually only live upstairs," he explained. "I'll get what I need and come straight back down."

"You live upstairs?" exclaimed Oliver surprised. "Since when?"

"Not long, look it doesn't matter. It's just a coincidence that we both live in the same block, that's all."

But it was very much far from a coincidence that Jay was living right upstairs from him.

And with that, Jay left Oliver and his mother for several minutes whilst he dashed upstairs to fetch the few bits that he needed.

In his apartment, he debated whether he should remove his cap, hair piece and coloured contact lenses. Oliver trusted him now and he deserved to know the truth. He deserved to know who Jay really was.

It had been too long now for both of them to be kept in the dark.

He took out his coloured contact lenses. He wouldn't be able to sleep in them anyway, so they had to go; that was an easy decision to make.

He took off his cap and removed his hair piece, revealing the much shorter crop underneath which he ran his fingers through and ruffled up slightly. He liked the slightly messy look.

He looked at himself in the mirror, he felt that he was a handsome young man; maybe it was time to stop covering it up once and for all.

Maybe it was time to be free.

Not only did Oliver deserve to know the truth, but he deserved to be able to show him the truth too.

He took a chance and decided to bear his true self.

When he returned downstairs, Oliver was already in his bed and his Mother was standing watching him at the bedroom door as he slowly began to drift into a peaceful and restful sleep.

Jay did not enter the bedroom; he simply stood behind Oliver's Mother and peered inside briefly before making himself comfortable on the settee underneath the spare bedding.

Oliver's mother gently closed the bedroom door on her son and let him sleep.

After returning to the living room / kitchen / dining room she spoke openly to Jay, and she was not one bit surprised by his sudden appearance changes - for they had already both been very open with each other and she knew exactly who he was, even if her son did not.

"Thank you for looking after my boy and for being here for him," she said, kneeling down to hug him once more. "I just want you to know that I think you would make a wonderful son-in-law."

"I hope so," he replied, "because I do love him and that is why I am here."

"I know you do," she said, wiping away several tears that had formed at the corner of her eyes, "and I'm sure he knows it too. But for now good night, my Angel."

"Good night," he replied, before snuggling back down underneath the spare bedding.

And after Oliver's mother had left, and the lights were all turned off, Jay whispered through the darkness to an unaware Oliver.

"And good night to you too, my Angel," he said.

And his heart was finally filled with hope for a better future.

2 days after Bonfire night

Robert (AKA Wendy) was up and at it quite early the next morning. He was most definitely one bird that wanted to catch his worm.

Keep fit, exercise
It helps reduce one's thunder thighs

"Come along, James," he hollered on the landing, whilst banging on his son's bedroom door to wake him up. "Let's get out there for a bit of a jogging."

"No thank you," replied James (AKA Tequila) from behind his closed door.

He knew that a bit of jogging was to be taken literally. Robert could barely walk up East Green Street without stopping for a breath or a cake, and the last time they jogged together he didn't even make it to his old studio flat.

Every now and again, Robert would go through this process of trying to lose weight because in the late summer he lost four pounds after a short stint of food poisoning which combined with a very tight belt under his belly hang over almost gave the illusion of a waistline.

Of course both Robert and Wendy exclaimed to all and sundry that he had been away on a detoxification and didn't he now look simply divine?

But inside his tiny bedroom, James was too busy trying to stuff just one more Tequila outfit into one of his three suitcases without the zips ripping open and the buckles pinging off.

He didn't have time for keep fit; besides he had already packed all his man clothes and he had nothing else to wear except for what he intended to travel in. Plus he was very mindful of Mark's warning not to leave the pub until the taxi arrived.

James had already checked his bank account online and true to his word; Mark had transferred over a generous amount of ill-gotten gains with his name written all over it. It was more money than James had ever had before and it would most definitely set him up nicely for his new life aboard.

He was feeling tired for he had barely slept the night before; he knew he probably wouldn't settle but it would all be worth it.

"Come on, James," hollered Wendy once more from the landing. "Get your tracksuit on. Wear the one I bought you that used to belong to that gangly black man at the Olympic Games, and I will wear its twin."

Two, four, six, eight
Exercising feels great

"You go on ahead without me," James replied.

He just couldn't believe that he would be in Gran Canaria that evening; it really was a dream come true. And if it didn't work out then so be it. He was young and ambitious and had a wad of cash to exploit.

After all, you only live once, right?

Out on the landing, Robert began running on the spot, well, more of a splotch on the carpet where he had recently dropped a jacket potato with chili con carne.

He hollered out to James just once more. "We stars of the show must look after our figures," he exclaimed. "And perhaps when we return we could do that new workout DVD I bought, you know the one: Shoo-size with Shimmy from 'The Black Queen'. And then we can enjoy a nice breakfast smoothie together too."

Behind the door and now sitting on his suitcase to close it, James smiled to himself. "No, thank you," he finally replied. "I can't stand Miss Shimmy Shoo, and the last time you made a breakfast smoothie you liquidized breakfast cereal and sausages together."

"Track suit yourself," replied Robert, and James could hear him running down the stairs and soon to be out of the front door.

James squeezed the third suitcase under his bed frame alongside the other two and pulled down the valence sheet to cover it all up. Everything looked as it should do and would not raise any suspicion should nosey prying eyes try to sneak a peek for anything untoward.

He then moved to the small window and looked at the world outside. This would be the last time that he would look through the glass down onto East Green Street and across the rooftops all around.

He saw Robert run a few steps down the pavement and then stop for a few deep breaths. He bent in half as the exercise stitch probably took over. He stayed there, watching his Father. It would be the last day they would spend together for quite some time.

Robert was really not what you would call a conventional Father but James would miss his deluded quirks, and as Mark had pointed out the previous day he could always come and visit once he had sorted himself out. It sounded like he was going to be staying in a nice complex out there which would be good to show off.

Down on the street, Robert stood up with his hands on his hips gasping for breath, and as he glanced back towards the pub and scanned the windows, he could see James watching him.

"Oh buggar," he exclaimed, and summoned up the strength to run a several more metres as though he was that Olympic champion who had 'once owned' the tracksuit he was wearing.

Five, four, three, two, one
Some things are best not done

James continued to watch from the window. It was funny. He knew exactly what his Father was playing at. He just wanted to see how long it could last for. Guaranteed, there would not be another sudden blast of second wind.

But unbeknown to any of them, there would be a blast of wind, and an unexpected one at that for the winds of change were really blowing through that morning.

And they intended to bring chaos and destruction with them.

Then suddenly, through his window, James saw a man approach Robert.

"Are you Wendy WolfWhistle?" he asked Robert.

"The one and only," replied Robert proudly.

"Yes, I can see that you are. You really don't look much better as a man or a woman, do you?"

"I beg your pardon?" remarked Robert.

Surely he must have greatly misheard that one?

"I implied that you look bloody awful."

"Do I know you?" asked Robert, most put out by this person's unwanted feedback.

"You should do," he replied, "we used to be best friends."

Robert stopped to think about that one. Hmmm, he had been best friends with just about everybody he knew. Perhaps it needed narrowing down just that little bit more.

And then along East Green Street came Mark (AKA Connie).

He was running as fast as he could to catch up with the person whom he had been referring to as The Arrival, before it all kicked off.

But he arrived too late for the shouting and screaming had already begun.

And it wouldn't be long before the curtains along East Green Street would begin to twitch and the whole street was awake.

And the winds of change were raging now.

Watch your back
Reset your mind
Leave your paranoia at the door
Somebody will shortly take their final breath upon the floor…

2 days after Bonfire night

There was an almighty racket going on in the street outside. What was going on? There was all manner of shouting and mayhem going on out there.

Wearily, Oliver pulled back the curtains that he had not yet replaced and peered out of his first floor flat window. He was quickly joined by Jay who had been woken up by all the screaming and shouting too.

They stood side by side and staring forwards, so Oliver did not notice that Jay looked different.

It seemed to be Robert and somebody else, both really going for it; airing their dirty laundry for all the street to hear and it seemed as though the curtains of the entire world were twitching to get a load of this one.

After all, a full throttle argument in the middle of their street was not an everyday encounter around these parts.

Not on East Green Street anyway, although it was never without its dramas.

"It's Wendy, I mean Robert; he's in trouble. We'd better go and help him," said Jay.

"Who is that with him?" asked Oliver, staring at the person who was verbally letting rip at him.

In the distance, Oliver could see somebody running towards the hot spot. He must have heard the commotion and believed he could intervene between the two.

It looked like Mark from Divas.

He used to be Miss Connie Lingus.

Was it really him?

Was he back?

Where had he been all this time?

Whoever it was, he was trying to pull whoever it was off Robert, but they were not having any of it.

They refused to be pulled off.

From Mark's perspective, The Arrival could not be moved.

Oliver noticed James (AKA Tequila) also running into the equation too. He must have heard the commotion from the pub and ran down the street to help his Father. If that is indeed what he was calling him these days.

Some days it fluctuated between Robert, Wendy, Father and Him.

"Come on," said Jay, reactively grabbing one of Oliver's coats on the way out; partly because it would be chilly out there and partly because he was only wearing his pyjamas.

Looking down at himself, Oliver realised he was not in any fit state to be seen in public, but did he have time to change? The T-shirt he had been wearing in bed would be fine, but he would have to pull on some jeans and footwear first.

"Right behind you," he finally said, but he slipped into the bedroom first to make some very quick necessary adjustments to himself.

By the time he was done and had found the time to have another peek out of the window, Jay was already out in the street helping to calm down the situation.

Oh, where had his longer hair gone?

Realising there was not much more to see and knowing that the idiots out on the street would soon be gone, some of the curtain twitching stopped and people returned to the dullness of their own lives.

Out on the street, Jay could hear the young man who had ran up the street telling one of them to go back to the hotel with him and calm down.

He was talking to Miss April Showers from 'The Black Queen', albeit out of drag and with short hair, but him none-the-less.

"What's going on here?" Jay demanded to know.

"This is the bitch that exposed me as a psychic fraud," replied April, referring to Robert, but looking directly at Jay. "Besides, what are you doing here?"

Oliver ran out of his front door and onto the street and joined them. "Is everything okay out here, Jay?" he asked.

"Oh, I get why now," added April, spotting the cutie that had followed him out of the nearby apartment block. "Nice."

"Do you two know each other?" asked Oliver.

"Just from some other place," replied Jay, before April could even contemplate giving an answer.

He didn't want April saying anything that might jeopardise what was organically developing between himself and Oliver. He felt they were already falling in love or at least he hoped they might be.

He certainly was at least.

Any blast from his past might certainly impact upon the situation. Negatively or positively it would go one way or the other but he didn't want to risk it either way.

The line was drawn and he was living for the here and now. A life which he very much hoped would always include Oliver.

Jay looked at April who understood that nothing more was to be said about it.

Oliver stared hard at Jay. How had he not realised that he was hiding beneath a mask?

"Are you okay?" Mark asked Robert, who was already receiving support from his son James.

"I'm fine," he replied. "Look, we'd better get off the road."

"And you had better get back inside," Mark whispered sternly into James's ear.

"Is that The Maniac?" James whispered back, pointing to the man who had been attacking his Father.

"No, it's April Showers from 'The Black Queen'," replied Mark.

And that is when it happened, just like last time.

Exactly like last time.

Exactly how Oliver always remembered it; every single day and every single night.

The car came out of nowhere.

The force of the impact caused the body to shift quite dramatically, to turn and fall hard to the ground below.

There was nothing anybody could have done to help him. There hadn't been time to react. It had all happened too fast. It was out of their hands.

Fate had intervened and had dealt the unluckiest of cards in combination:

The Day of Judgement.

The Tower of Destruction.

The Death card.

And the much dreaded Queen of Broken Hearts.

2 days after Bonfire night

Screams could be heard right along East Green Street as the car drove past at speed and quickly disappeared from sight.

The body was damaged; trembling; beyond repair.

Oliver...

James...

Robert...

Jay...

April...

Mark...

Demands for an ambulance to be called were prominent and almost deafening.

The curtains started twitching again. Now what had they missed?

Oh, another car accident. Hmmm, like they hadn't seen one of those before.

People all around fell to their knees and surrounded the fading body; inspecting the situation; trying desperately to make best judgements, any judgements, on what to do or say; requesting information that was barely incomprehensible and potentially of very little use.

Nobody was a medic and nobody knew what to do.

They needed that ambulance to come.

They needed the paramedics to breathe life back into him.

Who had done this? Who was responsible?

Chris Randall?

The Maniac?

Who?

Blood spilled quickly across the asphalt, but it was the head that had been most severely damaged.

The body was weak, very, very weak.

Somebody must have seen who was driving that car?

Anybody?

Every second that the ambulance did not arrive, the sparkle, the light, the soul was leaving the trembling figure on the ground.

He was dying and he knew it. They all knew it and there was nothing they could do to save him.

He stared at the sky as his brain, mind and body began to shut down.

He could feel it happening.

He could feel the life draining from his very existence.

This was the end, it really was, and this is how it felt.

He couldn't remember the sky ever looking so blue before as he lay on the cold, cold road.

> *Let me fly across the blue*
> *And maybe when I dream*
> *I will dream of you*

This is not how it should have been, not like this, not now.

He looked at the faces staring down at him and felt their concerns. He had hopefully made an impact; enough for all these people, at that moment, to care about him.

That was a nice thought to die with.

He closed his eyes.

And he knew that they would never, ever open again.

> *And what happens now?*
> *If I burn my bridges this time*
> *There can be no turning back now*
> *O peaceful sleep...*

Oliver...

Who always seemed to take the wrong turning at every crossroads and who destiny seemed to love to hate.

James...

Just about to embark on an exciting new adventure abroad, and with a pocket full of cash too.

Robert...

Soon to discover that Wendy would be made the sole headlining act of The Queen's Legs cabaret show.

Jay...

Who was finally filled with hope for a better future.

April...

Who could now put the ghosts of the past to rest and get on with his life, whichever way the wind blows.

And then there was Mark...

Who only returned to this god-forsaken town to right the wrongs he had caused before returning to his life of peace and solitude on the south coast.

The ambulance arrived.

The paramedics did everything they could, but it was not enough.

And then he took his final breath on this Earth.

And he slipped away to Heaven, where he belonged.

Oliver...

James...

Robert...

Jay...

April...

Mark...

Who?

And now... a short intermission

"Hi there, I'm Miss Shimmy Shoo and you probably best know me from starring in 'The Black Queen'.

"Today, I will be answering questions from just a few of my fans, just a few of my many, many fans.

"Yes, even more than you have Miss Lolita Lollypop. Oh, and don't think I don't know what you've been saying about me during your little back-street pub tour #notfunny. FYI, I'm only half a Hunty and you're the other half.

"Right, well my first question is from Rebecca in Devon.

"Rebecca really wants me to know that she loves me very much. Of course you do; all my little shoo shines do. I expect you're my biggest fan and I bet you wear your makeup exactly the same as mine, don't you?

"Well, Rebecca has a very long list of questions and no, I won't answer them all. This isn't *Mastermind*, you know - specialist subject me. Right Rebecca asks..."

Do you idolise anybody and if so why?

"Yes, I do idolise somebody... me, of course, and why me... because I'm fabulicious, that's why. And if you 'Shimmy it up' #shimmyitup, don't you know, you too can be as fabulicious as me."

Would you ever go out and have full on surgery or breast implants?

"Darling, when the package is delivered first class every time with a beautiful big bow on the top then there is no need to improve upon perfection, don't you think?"

Do you speak any other languages?

"Honestly Rebecca, I feel as though I'm forever speaking a different language from everyone else. I mean why does the world still insist on wearing those awful grey tracksuits, what the hell is that all about?

"I have spoken about them time and time again in my magazine column and during intimate chat-shows, but it's like nobody is listening to me. Just like in the reality TV house when I kept telling Anna Phylactic how nasty her dresses were, and her shoes, and her wigs... Oh just everything. You must know what I mean; I presume you saw the show.

"And in relation to another of your many and endless questions about whether or not I would like to work in fashion... Yes, I would. I'd ban the tracksuit. Please sign my online petition.

"Right, one more question from Rebecca and then I'm moving on to somebody else. You've already had far too much of my time and you're starting to bore me."

Have you ever had an affair with somebody famous?

"Darling, if you want to know the answer to that, then you're going to have to go out and buy my autobiography '*If the Shoo fits wear it*', which I believe may still be available in participating retailers. Is it? ... Yes, it is. Oh, I thought it would have sold out weeks ago because it is all about me.

"Right who is next? Okay it's Jan from Down Under. Down under what, Jan? Do you mean like that secret underwater city that they named the Atlantic sea after?"

Shimmy you are so gorgeous, why do you feel the need to belittle people? Is it because you have no self-confidence?

"No, Jan it's not. If I belittle people or appear to be doing so, then it's only because they are doing everything wrong. Believe me, this would be a much better world if everybody would just let themselves 'Shimmy it up' a bit.

Shimmy who or what would you be without your wigs?

"I would be a man that is what I would be. But a man, I hasten to add, in a stunning frock and with immaculate makeup from the *Made by Shimmy Shoo* range, of course.

"Right, are we done now can I go yet? I'm having that recurring dream analysed later. You know the one where I enter a reality TV house and I don't win.

"No, sorry, not dream analysis; counselling."

Q♥ CHAPTER 45 Q♥

2 days after Bonfire night

"...But first tonight, breaking news just in: A local man was knocked down by a car which then drove off at speed. The incident happened on East Green Street earlier today.

"He was treated at the roadside for multiple injuries before being taken to the Royal City Hospital. He was pronounced dead upon arrival.

"Police are appealing for witnesses or anyone with any information to contact them.

"The man has been named as Jay Galling, but perhaps better known as Miss Robyn RedBreasts from the television reality show 'The Black Queen'.

"Fellow star Miss April Showers was with him when he passed away. April told us: 'I can't believe this has happened. Robyn was the favourite of so many fans in the reality house.

"In my eyes, he was the real winner of The Queen of Spades.

"Now he will forever be known as The Queen of Broken Hearts. He is truly going to be missed by so many'.

"Our deepest sympathies go out to his family and friends on this very sad day."

A LEGACY OF GUILT

Today could be our final day
So the prophecies all say
If it's written down for all to see
Must we presume it's true?

Another sad love song on the radio
Another life lost on the news
Another storm
Another wave has washed away a town
And the tears that are falling
Just won't stop falling down

What are you leaving me?
I'm not responsible
Are my eyes deceiving me?
I'm not accountable
What are we fighting for?
I'm not invincible

And half the world is hiding
And half is still at war

Somehow, we're living in fear now
Afraid of the political row
Can we afford to change our minds?
Have the decisions all been made?

Another sad story on the TV
Another desperate heart-felt plea
Another war
Another gone, another bound to die
And the tears keep on falling
When will they all run dry?

What are you leaving me?
A legacy of guilt
Are my eyes deceiving me?
I'm blinded by the truth
What are we fighting for?
My strength has all but gone

And half the world is lonely
And half is all alone

I can hear the angels crying
Filling up the rivers and the oceans
With their tears
As they sit there softly sighing

I can hear them whispering your name
Calling you back home to Heaven
Where you belong

Why are you leaving me?
I'm not responsible
Have my eyes been deceiving me?
I'm blinded by the truth
Now I know what we are fighting for
The war is far from done

And half the world is lonely
And half will die too young

Sometime after the car accident

He had instantly become the most hated man in Britain.

He had killed one of the nation's sweethearts: Miss Robyn RedBreasts from 'The Black Queen'.

The nation had adored her, adored watching her and wanted to offer her luck and encouragement and help her on the road to finding love and success, but now they couldn't.

And all because of That Man.

He had wanted what he didn't have. He had wanted to reign supreme but now that dream was over and due to his negligence and his bad decisions another dream was well and truly over too.

A million dreams, if not more, were over.

Everybody who had ever dared to hope for love was hurt by this.

Anybody who dreamed of being different and accepted now felt destroyed.

A role model, ambassador and friend was gone, and all because of That Man.

And the nation had all come together to despise him.

And oh, how they all hated That Man.

There was no denying who he was. There were witnesses and CCTV footage to identify him.

The jury would find him guilty of murder and he would be locked away inside those four walls, for many years to come.

The outside world would be free of him. They would be safe from him.

There would be no repercussions for those who had stepped forward and spoken up.

That Man, he would become a prisoner of the past.

Forgotten, left to rot, alone and broken.

He was arrested shortly afterwards and taken into custody. He was led along the corridors by the officer with the moustache and taken through doors that locked tightly behind him.

He was led to a cell where he sat down on the bottom bunk and the door was locked behind him.

He would wait here until his trial, but he was guilty as charged for kidnapping Oliver and keeping him hostage potentially to die and for killing Jay; all that left to be seen was the length of the sentence.

A life for a life, no doubt.

He stared at the metal sink and toilet, the television and the messy walls. His eyes fixed firmly on the initials scratched into the walls, in particular the initials CR.

Chris Randall...

This was it, he had lost. He had failed to achieve, failed to gain the lead; failed to win the league.

Every card from this point onwards was a losing card. Every game played was a unanimous defeat.

Pick up two.

Pick up five.

Change direction.

Busted!

Game over!

Go directly to jail...

He continued to stare at the initials on the wall CR... CR... CR... CR... CR... CR...

Eventually, when he blinked, he could see the initials flashing in front of his eyes without even looking at them.

CR... CR... CR... CR... CR... CR...

Chris Randall...

***

There in front of him was the opportunity he had been waiting for.

There in front of him was an open door that would lead him right out of there.

The door to his freedom.

Suddenly, everything changed. Different sirens began to roar around the high walls of the complex. Action was finally being taken to stop all of this. They would swoop around the building and attack from the outside in. The world was taking control again. The riots would soon be over.

The atmosphere instantly changed and momentarily so did his chain of thought.

But the door to his freedom remained open.

However, this was a limited opportunity. It wouldn't be available for much longer, perhaps just a matter of seconds, if that.

He walked ever closer to it, knowing that time was no longer on his side.

It was now or never.

His freedom was calling him.

It was his for the taking.

The door to his freedom.

Time was really running out.

He continued to walk forward, quicker and quicker.

The door to his freedom.

The door to his past.

The door to his present.

The door to his future.

It was the door to his freedom.

He could hide on the outside; maybe even in disguise.

Yes, it was all his for the taking.

And he chose...

But Chris Randall did not choose to take it, not any of it.

He was not that stupid. If he escaped now it was unlikely he would ever stand a chance of getting out of there in a timely manner.

He walked away from the open door and back towards the prison building.

The riots would soon be over; soon he would be safe once more and he would help clean up the mess and the debris that he didn't create.

He would continue to show himself as being the model prisoner.

Surely it all had to go in his favour?

***

The prison door opened and in walked Chris Randall. The first thing he noticed was That Man sitting on his bunk bed.

"Well, didn't you make a massive fuck up of that then?" he remarked, ushering That Man off his bed. "It was Oliver I wanted, not Robyn RedBreasts. And don't think you can take me down with you because I won't let you."

He stared back at Chris, this had all been his doing but how was he ever going to convince anybody that he had all been a part of it too?

Yet again, the likes of Chris Randall had escaped their true destiny.

The likes of Chris Randall still needed lining up and shooting down.

But who would ever find the strength to do such a thing?

That Man stood up and suddenly the cell felt very claustrophobic with the two of them in there. He didn't know where to stand or what to do.

Were they now expected to live together and share a cell together?

Did he now have to wash and dress in front of him?

And go to the toilet in front of him?

Sensing his mood, fear and his apprehension, Chris offered some wise words of encouragement. "You'll get used to it all, and if you don't who cares? Besides, you'll probably be on your own soon enough."

And with that, Chris turned away and left the cell, leaving That Man to take it all in.

That Man...

Who was most definitely one phoenix that would not be rising from it ashes; not now and not anytime in the near, foreseeable or distant future.

That Man...

Who had nothing left bar the regret of ever putting their trust into Chris Randall to get what they wanted.

That Man...

Who had killed Jay Galling AKA Miss Robyn RedBreasts.

That Man...

Who would now never get his own pub again, for that is all that this had been about.

For That Man was Wayne.

Q❤ CHAPTER 47 Q❤

December

Oliver sat on the roadside kerb amongst the flowers and candles and poems that had been left by fans of 'The Black Queen' from near and far.

He stared out at where Jay Galling had died on the asphalt in front of him, the month before.

Jay, with whom he had once met briefly as Robyn RedBreasts when she had asked him out on a date with her ravishing self in front of all his work colleagues and had even tried to 'out' him too, even before he had really accepted himself that he was gay.

Jay, the guy who had never forgotten that they had met, had harboured feelings of love for him for months and months, and had saved his life because of this love.

Jay, who might have made him believe that perhaps he could love again.

Jay, whose name was now also forever engraved into his thoughts.

His Mother had been right. Her intuition had been spot on. He shouldn't have stayed here a moment longer. He should have left after they had sat together having coffee and cake in the old fashioned tea room where the staff looked twenty years older than they probably were.

There was no way he could stay here now though.

Not after this. Not anymore.

There was not one single reason to stay here anymore.

Not one.

But the winds of change had not yet blown away...

He had watched some scenes from 'The Black Queen' on the internet. It certainly seemed like a show he would have enjoyed watching and it would always be a wonderful moment in popular culture and a lasting memory to Jay Galling AKA Miss Robyn RedBreasts.

He hadn't watched much of it though; he hadn't been able to.

He saw just enough to have had a flavour of it and whilst high-maintenance and demanding characters like Miss Shimmy Shoo had almost raised a smile, it was overall very upsetting for him to watch.

One part in particular, stuck in his mind. Miss April Showers was giving psychic readings in the garden to some of them and she had told Robyn that she saw no future for her.

He couldn't quite remember now exactly what was said, but the whole scene retrospectively had been very distressing for him to watch.

He picked up a candle in a glass jar that he had left. The wax had run down and the wick had burnt out days ago. He smelt the jar and there was still just a slight aroma of raspberry;

both bitter and sweet, but red, just like the breast of a robin.

Yes, there was absolutely not one reason to stay here any longer.

He carefully put down the empty candle jar, although he really felt like throwing it as hard as he possibly could.

"Why does everybody I care about have to die?" he screamed out as loud as he possibly could. "And on this fucking road as well?"

"Hopefully not everybody does," replied a familiar voice behind him.

Startled, for he really thought he was alone, he turned around and gasped out loud.

The shock pushed him forward and he almost fell down to the floor. He had to put out his hands to regain his balance and composure.

For standing there, as real as he was, as alive as he was, was Jake Robinson.

And at that moment, the winds of change blew right through them both.

But Oliver had had enough...

COULD YOU LOVE ME ONCE AGAIN?

You were everything I ever wanted
So beautiful
Ethereal
You were everything I ever dreamt of
I never thought someone like you
Could love someone like me

I put you on a pedestal
So high that you could almost touch the sky
But I put you too far out of reach
And as time moved by
I stopped believing I was good enough for you

Fair of face
Style and grace
You once loved me with grand splendour
In a different time and place
You loved me then
I know you loved me then
Could you love me once again?

You were everything I ever needed
Sincerely
Loving me
You were everything my heart desired
You should have been the best of me
I should have realised

I lost my strength in loving you
It was the worst of times I can't relive again
But what is done can't be undone
Perhaps on that night, the stars were
misaligned

Fair of face
Style and grace
You once needed me beyond compare
In a different time and place
You loved me then
I know you loved me then

Could you love me once again?

And as the sun comes up
I wake up all alone
Can we turn back the hands of time?
So I won't be alone tonight

You loved me then
I know you loved me then
Could you love me once again?

Or is this the end of love?
Is this the end?

Is this the end of love?
Is this the end?

Is this the end?

Q💔 EPILOGUE Q💔

Out of sight, just around the corner of East Green Street, a pair of very cold, blue eyes peered through the shrubbery as Oliver and Jake were reunited for the first time in what seemed like forever.

It was Chris Randall.

He was finally a free man.

Legally, he was a free man.

And once more the outside world was his to rule again and he would start exactly where he stood; exactly where his destiny always seemed to bring him; East Green Street.

And to Jake.

And to Oliver.

And to every other bastard that had dared to play him at his own games and win.

But before he did anything else, before he saw anybody else, before anybody even knew where he was, he needed to make a visit to the Northern Territory.

He needed to begin his own negotiations...

Q♦ THE QUEEN OF DIAMONDS Q♦

The Queen of Diamonds.

The Queen of Coins.

Sometimes also known as The Queen of Pentacles.

Divinatory meaning: Generosity, wealth, desire, freedom.

If reversed: Fear, misguidance, abundance of evil.

How can the broken heart ever begin to heal when the devastation has only just begun?

How can the broken heart ever begin to heal when nobody knows who is next in line to fall?

How can the broken heart ever begin to heal and shine like a diamond?

Just like a diamond.

Like The Queen of Diamonds...

Keep up to date with The Queen of Diamonds and Tobias International at
www.facebook.com/tobiasint
Twitter @TobiasInt

CPSIA information can be obtained
at www.ICGtesting.com
Printed in the USA
BVOW08s1523240417
482096BV00001B/5/P